CAPTAIN COMBAT:
RED WINGS FOR THE BLOOD BATTALION

RED WINGS FOR THE BLOOD BATTALION

By Barry Barton

STEEGER BOOKS • 2021

CHAPTER 1
FOGS ARE FATAL

A FINE cold rain fell upon the streets of London, as though to add to the nerve rasping discomfort caused by the nightly blackout. From Highgate to Hammersmith the streets were practically empty. Even Piccadilly Circus, which in peace time is jammed with the upper crust, the lower crust, and the in-betweens, contained only four London bobbies and two Air Raid Wardens.

Down in Whitehall two men stood at the entrance to the War Office stamping their feet against the cold and cursing the war and everybody connected with it. Particularly Adolf Hitler. They were Scotland Yard inspectors and their job this night was to prevent anybody from entering the building who did not have a special right to do so. In all of London there were only thirty persons who held that special right, and at the moment they were up on the fourth floor seated about a massive oak table in the office of the Minister of War. They were the brains and guiding hands of England's forces.

It was a special meeting called to make plans and discuss ways and means of carrying them out so that Germany would be cracked three ways down the middle and peace returned to the world. On the morrow, as always happened, word would leak out of the secret meeting, and the press would howl to high Heaven for information of what took place, again the Sword

of Damocles, above the head of Prime Minister Chamberlain, would sway in the blast of criticism. But for tonight, however, it was a secret. The outside world would have to wait.

Grim as that meeting was it held little interest for the two Scotland Yard men down below for they were cold, and they had been assigned to secret meetings before. All they wanted the big shots to do was to hurry up and get it over with so they could return to the Yard and get warm again.

"Trust my blasted luck to be picked for this job!" growled the taller of the two. "For a penny I'd resign and get sent out to France."

"And you're speaking my very own thoughts," the other nodded. "From what I hear the Maginot Line is a pretty nice place to be. Moving pictures, hot water, the best food, and everything."

"And the safest place in the world right now," the tall one grunted. "A blasted queer war, I calls it. Back in Fourteen, France was the worst place to be in, but in this war it's the safest. Those Frenchies were no fools when they built that Maginot Line. Too bad that...."

"Stop a minute!" the short man suddenly snapped.

"Eh? What's up?"

The short man didn't answer for a few seconds. He rose up on his toes and cocked his head to one side and listened intently.

"I thought I heard a shot," he finally said.

"A shot?" the other gasped.

"It weren't no bloke sneezing!" the short man snapped. "We better step inside for a look around."

As though the gods were only waiting for them to push open the door, all hell suddenly broke loose from within the War Office building. Shots rang out and men cursed and shouted wildly. Feet thumped on the floors above and something made of glass and wood went crashing down a flight of stairs. And suddenly the lights went out and darkness rushed in with savage joy.

Their feet beating a rapid tattoo on the tiled ground floor, the two Scotland Yard men rushed for the stairs, each jerking a gun and a buglight from his pocket as he ran. When they hit the bottom of the stairs something hit them. A human projectile that sent them sprawling backward. As he went toppling over the short man managed to lock the fingers of one hand in the cloth of a coat. He hung on like a tiger and tried to jerk up his gun, but his gun hand was pinned under his own body.

"Got the beggar, Harry!" he choked out. "Give me a hand. Over this way, Harry! Give...."

The last was cut off sharply by the roar of a gun. A great white light exploded in the short man's brain, and he breathed his last in this world. The tall inspector's lunging body was already in the air as that gun roared. In the reflection of the spurt of red flame that streaked out from the muzzle of the gun he saw a wide flat face, small glittering eyes, and thick lips drawn back in a snarl. Then the reflection was blacked out and the Scotland Yard man's body went crashing down on the tiled floor.

His strong fingers clawed down a thick neck. He stopped their movement and tried to lock them about that neck and squeeze with every ounce of his strength. But the strength of the other man was more than equal to his. His hands were torn away, a fist smashed into his face, a gun barrel crashed down on his skull, and a hard knee drove viciously into his groin. White, searing pain engulfed him, and for a moment he could not move a muscle. With a desperate effort, however, he shook off the paralyzing effects and charged in anew.

THAT PRECIOUS moment, however, spelled his defeat. As he lunged once more he suddenly was stopped cold in mid flight and the crazy impression whipped through his brain that the entire building had fallen in on him. Like a sheet of paper in a gale of wind he was spun backward in the darkness. His body crashed against a wall, stopped, and crumpled, rubber-kneed, to the floor. In a painful daze he knew that the unseen killer was racing for the entrance doors. He could hear his running feet. He could hear running feet on the floor above, and the continued cries and shouts of men. He could hear and almost see them, but he could not move a single muscle of his body. His nerve centers had been stunned, and the agonizing paralysis held him prisoner.

As a dead man looking back at the living, he saw a moving shadow whisk out through the entrance doors and disappear. Then the lights came on. A group of men came pouring down the stairs. They looked wild eyed and very alarmed and frightened. They all talked at once.

"The devil got Sir Henry's briefcase!"

"And think what was in it!"

"Shot him right through the heart!"

"Which way did he go?"

"Did you see him?"

"Where is he?"

"Gad, look! The two guards. One of them's dead!"

"But Sir Henry is dead! That's important!"

"The press will make a great feast of this."

"We've got to hush it up, somehow."

"Think if we're forced to resign."

"Terrible!"

"My career ruined."

"Why the devil didn't these Yard men stop him? That's their job."

The Scotland Yard man tried to raise his hand, even a finger and point toward the entrance doors. But the only thing that moved was his heart, and it was beating slower and slower. He tried to talk with his eyes but nobody would look his way. They all milled around on the tiled floor like scared chickens clucking inanely.

"Did you see him? Just dashed in and snatched Sir Henry's briefcase."

"And shot him! Gad!"

"And dashed right out!"

"He might have shot any one of us, you know!"

"Gad."

"Somebody call the Yard!"

"This is terrible! My career...!"

CHAPTER 2
THE FURIOUS FUEHRER

B UILDING SHADOWS turned Berlin's streets into striped sticks of black and white candy in the growing twilight. Civilians on the sidewalks moved a bit faster than usual toward their homes because it would soon be dark and there were no street lights now that Germany was at war. A dark street is not safe in any city, but particularly unsafe in Berlin. One might meet a footpad, but he might also meet a Storm Trooper, or a member of the Gestapo, who hadn't slugged somebody in almost an hour. So naturally it was best to hurry home, stick the black sheets of paper on the window, and "relax" and wonder what in hell would be rationed next!

In a certain room in the Chancellery in Wilhelmstrasse, however, there were no shadows, no twilight, and no squares of black paper stuck over the windows. The room was ablaze with light that beat down upon the three men seated at a table. Two of them were known to the entire world. One was Herman Peiplow, supreme chief of German Intelligence, and trigger finger for The Great One. The other was the Great One, himself, in the flesh. The little guy with the little black nose wiper on his upper lip who some years ago had decided that he would be *Der Fuehrer*, and had made it stick ever since.

The third man at the table had a flat moon face, small glittering eyes, and thick lips. He also had the murder of two Scotland Yard Inspectors, and a British War Office potentate, on his conscience. Only he didn't have a conscience because *Der Fuehrer* would have you shot for possessing such a thing. Such things are for only God loving fools who would like to make something of the world… such as it is.

The third man at the table was speaking, and although his voice was brisk and business-like, it virtually dripped with triumph and pride, because he thought he was quite a fellow.

"They were all so busy talking of their foolish plans," he said, looking at the Leader, "not one of them saw me enter the room. *Gott*, for six days and nights I had been hiding in the building. I knew you would want what was in the briefcase of that Sir Henry. So I concentrated on it. When I shot him the others were too surprised, or scared, to make a move. With my other hand I snatched up the case and fled. It was very easy. Two of their Scotland Yard men tried to stop me, but they are very stupid fellows. And so...."

The man paused, gestured with one hand and smiled.

Captain Combat

"I hope I have pleased you, *Fuehrer?*" he murmured.

The head of the German Reich scowled at the mass of papers

before him. It was not his policy to give credit to others because that meant taking credit from himself.

"You have not failed, anyway," he finally muttered. Then jerking his head toward the door, "You may leave us, now. Perhaps I will talk with you later. Shoot a *Jüde* or two if you wish to enjoy yourself. I think you have earned that pleasure; at any rate."

When the spy had left, closing the door softly behind him, the German Leader looked once more at the mass of papers, and his eyes lighted up like those of a snake.

"This will be very useful to us, *Herr* Peiplow," he grunted. "Your man did a good job, but I think it would be a good idea for you to reprimand him. Mildly, of course."

"Then you are not pleased, *Fuehrer?*" the chief of German Intelligence asked in surprise.

"I could be more pleased!" the other snapped. "There were Chamberlain and Churchill in that room, and Eden, too. Your spy had more bullets in his gun, did he not?"

"Ah, yes," Peiplow breathed. "I will speak to him, *Fuehrer.* And now?"

The Intelligence chief paused and waited expectantly. The German Leader didn't answer for several moments. He bent over the maps, and code books, and secret reports that should be in London… only they weren't. After awhile he nodded his head, and drew a line with his finger on one of the maps.

"There," he said. "There is a good place to make an attack."

Peiplow bent over and looked at the map and his little black eyes almost popped out of his head. It was a couple of seconds before he could shake his tongue loose.

"*There, Fuehrer?*" he gasped. "The Maginot Line? *Himmel,* it would cost us a million soldiers to smash through there. Surely you don't mean to attack the Maginot Line?"

The German Leader turned his head and bored him with his eyes. The bloodthirsty, heartless Peiplow, the man who had had thousands slaughtered on his order, cringed before the icy stare.

"Was I not the greatest soldier Germany had in the last war?" the *Fuehrer* snapped. "Am I not the greatest German in the world today?"

"You are our Leader," Peiplow stammered hastily. "You will always be our Leader."

"Then hold your tongue, and listen until I have finished!" the *Fuehrer* grated.

Pausing a moment to puff up his flat chest a bit, and tickle his nose with the little black thatch on his upper lip, the German Leader continued speaking. Ten minutes later he leaned back and stared at Peiplow.

"Well, and what do you think, now, *Herr* Peiplow?" he demanded.

"It is perfect, *Fuehrer!*" Peiplow breathed. And there was awed admiration in his voice. "Only a brain like yours could have thought up such a clever plan. It will cost us some troops…."

"Unimportant!" the *Fuehrer* barked. "German soldiers are glad to die for me. It is their duty."

"It will not please the American countries," Peiplow murmured, his eyes on the map.

The German Leader laughed harshly.

"What will I care about them when this success makes me

ruler of all Europe?" he snorted. "Before they realize what has happened I shall have Asia, too! But first, I will crush England!"

"To crush England!" Peiplow breathed softly. "Gott, to set up my office in London would make me a very happy man, *Fuehrer.*"

"Within a week after I give the signal," the Leader said, "you will be able to do that. Perhaps in less than a week."

"And I shall make it my first job to find him," Peiplow grunted and stared off into space. "I only hope he will not be killed in the meantime. I have promised myself the great pleasure of doing that. The one perfect moment of my life when I do so, *ja!*"

"You speak words that make not sense, *Herr* Peiplow!" *Der Fuehrer* snapped.

"I speak of the swine called Combat!" Peiplow said in a voice that shook with hate. "The swine whose mother was English, and his father American. His father flew for the Americans in the last war, and was shot down. The son, William Combat, was born on Armistice Day. Two months ago he was here in Berlin, as you know, *Fuehrer,* with his mother. On your orders...."

"Yes, I know all about that!" the Leader cut him off. "You fools allowed him to escape the day before war broke out. True, you killed his mother, but not him. And he made a fool of you at Hamburg, too!"

"He will not do so again," Peiplow said softly. "And with your permission, *Fuehrer,* I have a suggestion to make."

"Then make it!"—

PEIPLOW TAPPED a thick finger on the map and squinted his black eyes. "Would it not be wise to give our enemies a faint inkling of our plan, *Fuehrer?*" he murmured. "Make them curious, to say nothing of alarmed? They will, of course, rush troops to France. Their agents will come into Germany. We will know of their arrival, of course. We can arrange to feed them with information we wish them to have. It will go back to the British War Office, of course. They, the stupid fools, will act accordingly. Then when you give the signal for *Der Tag, Fuehrer,* they will be trapped and utterly helpless. Is that not a good suggestion, *Fuehrer?*"

The German Leader gave him a twisted smile... scornful pity.

"Of course it is," he said. "But I had already thought of doing it. But there was another reason for making the suggestion, eh? And perhaps it has to do with this Captain Combat?"

"It has, *Fuehrer!*" Peiplow said viciously. "The English swine think of him as a very clever man. When they become alarmed wondering about your wonderful plan, *Fuehrer,* perhaps they will appeal to him to help. Perhaps they will send him over here to Germany. That is what I shall hope. I will know the minute he leaves. And when he arrives...."

The chief of German Intelligence stretched out his two hands and then slowly closed his fingers and twisted savagely as though a man's neck was in his grasp. The Leader watched him, and laughed.

"I think you will have that moment, *Herr* Peiplow," he said. "And I shall delight in watching you. Yes, we might just as well get rid of the swine dog at the first opportunity. Very well, then. Now where are those execution orders for Jews in Poland? I will sign them now, and then rest. I am meeting my army generals soon, and it tires me to listen to them prattle on how a war should be conducted. *I* know. They don't! *Gott,* no. So I shall tell them of my newest secret weapon, and perhaps allow a few of them to watch the first test!"

CHAPTER 3
MYSTERY WATERS

B LANKET AFTER blanket of cold and clammy fog rolled down from the Arctic wastes to cover the wind-whipped waters of the North Sea. It was bird-walking weather as far as the flying airplanes was concerned. But there was a war on, and when there is a war on, men must fly while there is even a foot of ceiling. And so, British Royal Air Force scouting patrols winged their ways out over the stretches of the North Sea. Some of the pilots flew low, just about skipping along the tops of the tossing waves. The others flew high, well up in the sunshine, above the strata of dank fog. But, whether low or high, each pilot and gunner kept his eyes skinned for the first glimmer of Nazi wings roaring out of the east and southeast.

Slouched comfortably in the pit of his high speed Hawker Hurricane, Captain Bill Combat stared fixedly toward the east and breathed a fervent prayer that the Nazis would take advantage of the fog and send some bombers out to pester, if not destroy, a bit of British shipping in the North Sea. For almost two months now, he had been assigned to bomber patrol work and had seen no more action than you could record on the back of a postage stamp. And action, action against Nazi airmen, was the thing he craved more than anything else in life. To blast square-headed Nazi pilots down into permanent oblivion was his sole desire, morning, noon and night.

Because that would help England? Because that would bring about a speedy peace? No! Not exactly. He wanted to see the wings of a Nazi plane in his sights, to see the bullets from his eight machine guns chew into it, because he hated the pilots of the Nazi Air Force beyond any words of mere description. He hated them individually and collectively because, the very day before Hitler had marched into Poland, Nazi pilots had killed his mother in cold blood. Killed her as he was in the very act of flying her out of Germany. It might be said it was a miracle he had not been killed as well. But he did not consider it as such. On the contrary he considered it an act of God; that he might go on avenging his mother's brutal murder until every last one of Hitler's flying butchers was buried deep under the sod, and filled with aerial machine gun bullets.

Yes, Combat wanted action above all else. And he wasn't getting any. True, like a good soldier, he did not complain to his superiors, but these daily patrols, with nothing to do except fly, were slowly getting on his nerves.

"Maybe I should get me transferred to the navy," he interrupted his thoughts aloud. "In this damn war it seems to be only sailors who see any action. Nuts, what's holding back these bums, anyway? Why don't they send over their bombers in flocks? Or do they realize we're all set to paste the hell out of them? Maybe they're just feeling around with two or three at a time, just to...."

He cut the rest off sharply and sat a bit straighter in his seat. A few miles ahead there was a wide break in the rolling fog, and as he had stared at it, he thought he caught the flash of wings, down close to the water. Of course, it might have been a shadow, cast by a small cloud, but….

"But it isn't!" he shouted suddenly, then banged at his throttle with a free fist. "It's a plane. A parasol type. And we don't have any of those jobs on this patrol work!"

As he spoke the words he slanted the ship's nose down and hunched forward over the stick, his eyes straining toward the break in the fog. Then suddenly he saw it again. It was a fairly small two-seater, high-winged monoplane. It was scooting along just over the tips of the waves, and the black swastika insignia of Hitler's hordes stood out in clear relief against the dull grey of the wing and fuselage. A moment later it had slid under the lip of the fog bank, then disappeared toward the north.

"It adds up to one of two things," Combat muttered and gunned his ship toward the break in the fog. "It's either some dumb greenhorn who has got himself lost, or else it's some lad off on a dizzy stunt."

That it could be a German greenhorn, lost on his second or third solo, seemed quite unlikely, if only because the plane was so far out over the North Sea. True, that type of plane, (it was a Henschel, powered with a BMW engine), had a fairly long cruising range, but just the same, it was used mostly for land work. And no matter which way you looked at it, the plane was definitely not the type suited for escort bomber work.

"So some lad is up to something," Combat finally summed it up. "So, here's where we have a look, anyway. We'll…."

ONCE AGAIN he let his voice trail off into silence and

stiffened in his seat. Off his right wing, some fifteen or twenty miles, and three or four thousand feet higher up than himself, a cluster of a dozen wings slid through the air in the general direction of England's coast. Too many times had Combat spotted German bomber wings in the air to miss them now. Just to make sure, however, he took a good look. Then he checked his position and glanced at the map panel fitted to the side of his cockpit. It contained a specially prepared map, marked off in a graduating series of squares. If a pilot knew his position, according to latitude and longitude, he could very easily "pin-point" the position of a ship at sea or a plane in the air, and send out in radio code, to his shore receiving station, exactly at what point the enemy craft had been spotted.

It only took Combat a minute or so to contact his base squadron and give the alarm. But every second of that time he kept his eyes on the bomber squadron. Suddenly, as though their commander had spotted him for the first time, the giant wings heeled over almost to the vertical; the bombers wheeled off their course and headed south. Combat stared at them in dumbfounded amazement.

"What the hell, yellow bellies?" he choked out impulsively. "Does one lone British plane scare the tar out of you?"

His shouted question was lost in the roar of his own engine, and there was no answer forthcoming. Then, to his added amazement, the squadron of German bombers split up into two separate sections. One section headed toward the English coast, while the other continued toward the south. Perhaps, in somebody's mind, it was a very clever aerial maneuver, but in Combat's

SIR JOHN BAKER

the split-up was as though the pilots were simply asking for trouble. The one thing attacking single seaters try to do to raiding bombers is to split them up. Yet those Hun pilots, undoubtedly knowing they had been spotted, and that planes were rushing out from shore to intercept them, had deliberately split up and were now flying off in two directions.

For a second or so Combat stared at them, then he glued his eyes on the nearest bomber, automatically checking his guns. Then he went into action. But that was all he did. He just started to go into action, for in that split second a thought flashed through his brain. Perhaps it was intuition, perhaps it was a man's natural suspicion that it is always trebled in war time, or perhaps it was just a hunch. At any rate, he suddenly cut away from the two sections of bombers and went spinning down toward the split in the fog.

"I could catch me a nice piece of hell for not slamming in for the attack," he murmured, brows furrowed, "but maybe their stunt was to pull me away from that Henschel job. Anyway, I gotta find out, just in case."

With a grim nod for emphasis he dived for the split in the fog and went thundering down toward the water. Perhaps the gods had decided to give him a break, because the fog at that point had mushed upward, giving a ceiling of some fifteen hundred feet, and with fair visibility. No sooner had Combat sliced into clear air than he spotted the lone Henschel, some fourteen or fifteen miles away. However, he spotted something else that instantly snapped his attention away from the parasol type of plane.

IT WAS another plane. A huge transport, and one swift glance showed Dutch airline markings on the cabin. It was just under the fog bank and flying at a very slow speed toward the north in the same direction as the Henschel two-seater.

"Of course I could be wrong," Combat grunted, "but I'm damned if I ever heard of Dutch Airlines flying a route to the North Pole. And that's certainly where that baby is headed… and no landing fields in between either!"

Completely puzzled for a moment, Combat peered hard at the transport. Then a third object caught his gaze. It was an old, storm-battered tramp steamer, pushing through the waters of the North Sea. From where he sat he could not make out the flag at the masthead, but there wasn't any painted flag and name on the side of the ship. So that made it a British ship, beyond question—just an old tramp caught in a distant port at the outbreak of hostilities, and now plowing through the last leg of its weary journey back home.

However, it was not the sight of the surface ship that held Combat's eyes. It was the Henschel slanting down toward it. The German plane was going down almost at the vertical, and for a moment Combat thought its pilot had gone nuts and was planning to sink it by diving right straight down through it. But, before that came to pass, however, the Henschel nosed out of its dive and began circling the small freighter.

Four times it curved around the boat. Then suddenly it roared straight ahead, cut back and streaked for the bow. Instinctively Combat waited to see the bombs spill down from the German plane, and unconsciously he cursed aloud and tried to urge his own plane to greater speed. No bombs went twisting down, however. The Henschel skipped by over the tramp, missing its masts by no more than a few feet. Then it zoomed upward and went streaking away toward the southeast. In spite of himself, Combat followed it with his eyes until he had lost it in the fog.

"The guy must be drunk!" he grunted.

"Of all the dizzy...."

Bill Combat never finished the rest of that sentence. Rather, he ended it with a wild shout of dumbfounded amazement. The little tramp steamer was still plowing valiantly onward, but from stem to stern it was a mass of flame that clung mysteriously to the craft like a hell shroud. The smoke that accompanied the flame was a sickly pale green. It was as though the tramp steamer had been slung by invisible hands straight into the yawning mouth of a smelting furnace, but had pushed out through a hole in the other side.

CHAPTER 4
WAR OFFICE CALLING!

"I'M SEEING things! I must be waking up after a terrific bender! My God!"

From a long ways off Combat's shouted words drifted back to him to penetrate his brain and snap him out of his trance. His eyes weren't playing him tricks, and he wasn't coming to the morning after a terrific bender. The tramp steamer on the water was a mass of flame. Even as he watched it the fire, apparently, had reached the boilers. A column of roaring hell spouted high up into the air. The ship broke in two, like a match between your fingers, water boiled and foamed, while great clouds of smoke blotted out the scene as the two halves of the boat went to their wet grave in the sea.

Slamming ahead at full throttle, Combat howled down toward the spot, hoping for sight of survivors in the water, but realizing in his heart that no one could possibly have lived through that awful hell. As disconnected thoughts raced through his brain, he automatically snapped on his short-wave transmitter and reported the sinking to his home base.

"We'll notify any surface craft in the vicinity, Captain," the operator at the other end said when he'd finished. "By the way, sir, we've been trying to contact you. Colonel Nevens' orders, sir. You are to quit your patrol at once and return to the Base."

Combat's heart skipped a beat, and he wondered how in hell his commanding officer could have learned he'd passed up attacking the bombers. It had to be that, because you were never called off patrol unless you had pulled a bad one, or were due for a medal and the King had arrived and was waiting to pin it on.

"And I haven't any medals coming to me," he whispered softly. Then in a louder tone, "Any idea of the reason, Operator?"

"None, sir," came the calm reply. "The Colonel simply gave me orders to contact you."

"Okay, signing off," Combat grunted. "I'll…."

He let out a yell. He had unconsciously taken his eyes off the still slightly boiling waters below him and glanced eastward, and, for the briefest part of a second, he had caught a glimpse of two planes flying southeast toward Helgoland and the German coast beyond. One ship had been the Henschel parasol, and the other had been the Dutch airliner.

It was just the glimpse of them, streaking through a thin stretch of fog. One glimpse, but Combat had reacted automatically. He pulled up the nose of his Hawker Hurricane, fed the engine every ounce of fuel it would take and went boiling up into that fog. A minute or so later he was above the stuff and scanning the heavens in all directions for sight of the two planes. Of course it might have been a case of the Dutch transport being lost, and the German pilot extending the courtesy due a neutral by leading him back to his native shore. However, for reasons Combat couldn't even explain to himself, he was sure that the Dutch plane was not lost. In fact he was possessed with a very strong hunch that the controls of that neutral plane were in Nazi hands.

"No!" he muttered and tried to do X-ray tricks with his eyes in the fog below. "No Dutchman was flying that crate. It was out

there to watch that Henschel and that tramp steamer. And…
and just what in hell did happen? There were no bombs, and no
torpedo… unless I'm going blind in my old age."

He let it go with a shrug, but temptation rode beside him,
taunting him all the way.

"Cut it!" he grated as his thoughts started to wander back in
memory. "You're wanted at Base. Do your thinking after you
get there… if the C.O. hasn't given you something else to think
about."

And so, with a certain amount of reluctance he gave up his
hunt for the two planes, obviously flying blind in the fog, and set
a course that would take him on a bee-line to his home base at
Hornsea on the English east coast. When he finally landed he
was a bit surprised to see that all the other ships of the squadron
were back from patrol and on the ground. It didn't take much
thinking to guess that they had not picked up the raiding bombers and so had returned.

When he entered the Squadron Office and saluted Colonel (Wing Commander) Nevens, his guess was proved to be
entirely correct.

"Was that alarm report supposed to be one of your crazy
American jokes, Combat?" the C.O. barked at him. "I ordered
the entire squadron out. They found nothing but water, fog,
and sky!"

"It was no joke, sir," Combat said in an even tone. "Right after
my call to you they split into two groups. One headed west and
the other headed south. They…."

"*What?*" the Wing Commander exploded Then in a more

23

soothing tone, "Come, now, Combat, you know perfectly well that bombers don't split up until the single seaters make them. What earthly reason…?"

"I was about to say, sir," Combat broke in coldly, "that I believe they broke up as a means of trying to make me go after one group or the other. In other words, to draw me away. I didn't fall for it, and as a result, I saw the damndest thing."

"Yes, your last report," the other nodded. "Tell me in detail. I think our operator got it all garbled up."

IN A few sentences that left out nothing of importance, Bill Combat reported his entire flight from start to finish. The Wing Commander listened in silence, but his eyes grew larger and larger, and the corners of his mouth twitched more and more. When Combat called a halt, the Wing Commander almost burst out laughing. With an effort he controlled himself, and gave the Yank born pilot a paternal smile.

"You youngsters go haywire when it comes to war," he chuckled. "Hear and see the damnedest things. There's only two ways an airplane can sink a surface ship, Combat. They either bomb it or they torpedo it. You just didn't see what happened, that's all. Ten to one that plane simply spotted it for a lurking U-boat and it was then torpedoed. You want to teach your fancy not to run wild in the future."

"Yes sir," Combat said quietly. But inside of him a voice roared, "Listen, you big stiff, speaking of war, just paste it in your hat that I've already nailed eight Hun planes while you've done nothing but polish your pants on the seat of a swivel chair. Don't tell me what I see!"

But naturally Combat simply said, "Yes sir," because even a politically appointed Wing Commander has the authority to get very tough with you and make things twice as unpleasant.

"That's the lad," the Wing Commander smiled. "Don't be discouraged, Combat, there are a lot of funny things in a war. Now, about the reason I sent for you to return. I received a phone call a couple of hours ago. From Air Ministry. You are to fly to London at once, and report to Sir John Baker at the War Office. Is Sir John a relative of your mother's by any chance, Combat?"

The Yank shook his head. "Not that I know of, sir," he said.

"Oh, just wondering, of course," the other smiled and gave a little wave of his hand. "Sir John is a pretty big man in the Cabinet, and the War Office. No idea, I suppose, why he'd want to see you?"

"Not the faintest, sir," Combat said.

That, however, was not exactly the truth. Sir John Baker had been a close friend of his mother's brother, Sir Henry Brainbridge, chief of British Intelligence on the Continent. Sir John and Sir Henry had worked together in Intelligence work. Sir Henry had died in Combat's arms on a park bench in Posen, Poland. Died from the Nazi secret agent's rifle bullet that had been meant for William Combat's heart. And so a few minutes later, when the Yank left the Wing Commander's office and prepared for his flight to London, he wondered why Sir John had sent for him and felt sure his guess was close to the truth—that there were other things ahead in the immediate future other than just routine North Sea patrol work.

CHAPTER 5
MAGINOT MENACE

SIR JOHN BAKER immediately put down the newspaper he was reading and rose to his feet as Bill Combat was ushered into the office. The Cabinet member's smile of marked relief was in direct contrast to the worry in his tired eyes as he grasped Combat's hand.

"I'm glad to see you, William," he said. "Take that chair there. A cigarette, eh?"

"Thank you, Sir John," Combat said and dipped a hand into the ornate ivory box the other held out. "I came right down as soon as I received word. I hope it…."

The Yank stopped short as his eyes fell on the newspaper Sir John had been reading. The banner headline seemed to leap right up off the first page to smack him between the eyes. It read:

Churchill Tells House Royal Oak Was Torpedoed at Scapa Flow

His fingers still in the ivory cigarette box, Combat sat as a man struck dumb, gaping at the headline. It was difficult to believe his eyes. Naturally, like everybody else in the world, he knew that the British ship of the line had been sent to her doom by a German submarine with a loss of over eight hundred officers and men. But also, like everybody else, he had believed the vessel was nailed on the high seas. To learn the ship had been caught at anchor in Scapa Flow, England's most famous naval base, located in the Orkney Islands, off the northern tip of Scotland, was as startling as to have your best friend suddenly haul off and pin your ears back.

"You were about to say, you hope it is nothing serious, William?" Sir John murmured. "I mean for my sending for you? I'm afraid it is. Yes, very serious, indeed."

Combat raised his eyes and nodded at the newspaper spread out on the desk.

"That's true?" he asked with an effort. "A U-boat actually slid through the defenses of Scapa Flow?"

"It's true, and it did," Sir John nodded solemnly. "And I have enough sporting blood in my veins to salute the commander of that craft for a very daring bit of work. However, his task was somewhat simplified because he knew the exact location of every mine boom and submarine net in the Flow."

"For cat's sake!" Combat gasped. "You mean…?"

"I mean that we are in a deuce of a mess, William," the other interrupted. "To use one of your American expressions, we are on our ear and right out on the end of the limb. You remember reading about the death of Sir Henry Carter three weeks ago?"

"Shot by a footpad trying to rob him, wasn't he?" Combat asked. Then he added, "Frankly, I didn't quite swallow that story."

"Nor did anybody, I fancy," Sir John said with a grimace. "It was foolish not to publish the truth, but… Well, let us say the Minister of Information has his own ideas. Incidentally, I suspect you'll see a change in that department presently. However, the truth is that Sir Henry was shot and killed by a Nazi agent while attending a secret War Council meeting, right here in this building. His brief case was stolen, and among the things it contained was a complete map of the defenses of our naval bases, including Scapa Flow. Why the defenses weren't changed at once is something I cannot explain, for I can't understand it, myself. However, Scapa Flow wasn't. I hope that now a certain gentleman has learned a lesson. A most costly lesson in English blood, I might add."

Combat made no comment as Sir John finished. He had done two weeks of training service on the Royal Oak and had a host of friends among her officers. Now she was at the bottom of Scapa Flow, and perhaps all of his friends were down there with her. Damn wars to hell, and the people who run them!

"This will cause quite a stink," he finally said.

"I only hope to God it isn't just the beginning," Sir John groaned. "But I think we'd better get down to the reason why I sent for you, William. As you know, your late uncle, Sir Henry Brainbridge, was my dearest friend. He was very fond of you, and admired you greatly. Of course I know all about your splendid achievements at Hamburg during the first few days of the war. And of how you carried out your uncle's dying request."

Sir John paused, avoided Combat's eyes, and looked slightly embarrassed. The Yank instantly took steps to clear the atmosphere.

"What I told you when I returned to England, Sir John, still goes," he said quietly. "I stand ready to tackle any job you feel he would want me to tackle. Anything, because I'm living on borrowed time for just one purpose… to help blast Nazism to a final fare-thee-well!"

"Thank you, William," the other said with a trace of husky

emotion in his voice. "I knew, of course, you would say that. But… well, heartless as I try to be at my job, it still is not pleasant to ask a man to walk out of this office to his death."

"We all catch it eventually, war or no war," Combat shrugged. "Naturally, no man *wants* to die, but… But, what the hell? What kind of a job have you got in mind, sir?"

"That's the deuce of it, William," the other said with a frown. "I just don't know, exactly. William, in that file behind you, there are over two hundred reports from British Intelligence agents inside Germany. Every one of them speaks of some plan the Nazis are hatching up. A plan that will end this war as quickly as the Polish war was ended. Now, don't mistake me, I'm not trying to throw a scare around. Particularly when I haven't got one shred of anything definite to go on. However, our agents are well trained. They are not sent soaring to the clouds by unconfirmed rumors. As a matter of fact, they do not put very many facts in their reports. Let us say they… well, that they feel something is brewing, now."

"I think I understand," Combat nodded. "I know what that feeling is like. What few facts have they given you?"

"One fact, and they all have forwarded it on, is that the Germans are manning the Siegfried Line to the hilt, and moving up countless troops and arms for support. I know what you're thinking. To smash the Maginot Line would cost Hitler over a million soldiers, perhaps two million. But bear this in mind. Hitler is a mad man. All the world admits that, so to hurl two million men to their death may mean nothing to him so long as the Maginot line is broken through. Perhaps he believes that we would sue for peace in the event German troops were once more overrunning France."

"It's a thought," Combat nodded slowly. "Somehow, though, it doesn't jell with me. To bust the Maginot line would be something, but it wouldn't mean German troops in England. At least not for quite awhile. And England is the one country Hitler hates most. No, I can't even see him tossing two millions of his dumb headed worshipers at the Maginot Line."

"Perhaps," Sir John said and shrugged. But the tone of his voice indicated he was far from being in agreement with Combat on that point. "Anyway, here is another small item that has filtered through. You have heard of the Breslau Works just outside Berlin?"

"I've even visited the plant," Combat said. "A couple of years ago. They were developing and experimenting with an airplane wing dope for both fabric and metal that would be not only fireproof but completely weather resisting. It was hoped it would add to the repair life of ships flying in the tropics and the Far East. As I recall, the German Bureau of Military Research took it over about six months before the war."

"Correct," Sir John nodded. "Breslau is one of the finest chemical works in the world. Anyway, the report has come through to me that every man and woman at the plant has been more or less imprisoned in it. They have to eat, work, and sleep within its walls. No contact with the outside world is permitted. They cannot even see their relatives, much less write to them. There is also a cordon of guards that circle the place. Anyone, even a German, is shot on sight if he or she approaches the works.

Let me add that two of my best agents met their deaths when they went there under the guise of skilled men applying for work."

SIR JOHN paused and scowled. Then he slowly heaved a long sigh and shook his head.

HERR PEIPLOW

"There is a third one of my agents inside the place," he said after awhile. "They were trying to get inside and contact him. They...."

"How did that third man get in?" Combat interrupted with the question.

The Cabinet member smiled sadly.

"He didn't do it after they made the place a prison," he said. "He was in there before the German Government took it over. Naturally, during the last two or three years, we've had agents working in most of the industrial centers of Germany. Every one of their reports was presented to Mr. Chamberlain before the Munich Conference last year. But the Prime Minister...."

"Was a most ardent lover of peace," Combat said grimly.

"Anyway, it's ancient history," Sir John murmured. "We've got a war on our hands, so it doesn't help to talk of what could have been done. However, shortly before Germany marched into Poland my agent in the Breslau Works managed to get word out that he needed help. The message finally reached me about tenth hand, I guess, and was rather garbled. I was positive, however, that he had something by the tail, and so I've been trying to contact him ever since. And have lost four men in the attempt."

"Have you any definite reason for linking up the Breslau Works with any plan the Nazis are hatching up?" Combat asked.

"Yes," Sir John replied at once. "We caught a Nazi agent here in London a couple of days ago. He had some papers on him. One was a coded message from Hermann Peiplow. It...."

"The Chief of German Intelligence!" Combat said sharply and his brain raced back in memory to highly unpleasant things. "That louse!"

"Knowing that particular code, our Cipher Bureau was able to break it down," Sir John continued. "It was an order from Peiplow to the agent to clear up his affairs in London at once and return to Germany to serve as liaison officer between Colonel Stoltz and General von Maken."

"Von Maken?" Combat shouted. "He's the general in command of the Siegfried Line forces!"

"Yes, of course," Sir John said quietly. "And Colonel Stoltz is the man Hitler put in charge of operations at the Breslau Works."

Combat whistled softly and the gleam of tensed excitement leaped into his eyes.

"That's a definite link, all right," he said. "And your man inside the Breslau Works probably knows all the answers, but can't get them out to you."

"That is my belief," Sir John murmured. Then with a grimace, "*If* he is still alive. That's what annoys me most, whether he is alive or dead. It makes me feel pretty awful to think that possibly I've sent four men to their deaths, looking for a man who was already dead, himself."

"That's a chance you can't help but take," Combat said sympathetically. "If that agent is alive and we could get through to him somehow...."

"*We?*" Sir John echoed with a faint smile.

"Didn't you send for me, Sir John?" Combat asked bluntly.

"Perhaps I wanted your opinion on the matter," Sir John said.

"Well, if that's the case," Combat said with a grin, "my opinion is that I think you have something in this agent at the Breslau Works. And I also think it would be a swell idea if you'd let me take a crack at trying to get through to him."

"How would you propose to do it?" Sir John asked.

Combat didn't answer for a moment or two. He lighted another cigarette, then leaned back in his chair and with eyes closed, studied the map of Berlin and its surroundings pictured on his brain. Presently he began talking, but he kept his eyes closed. It was as though he were speaking his thoughts aloud to see how they sounded in the open air.

"The Breslau Works cover an area of about five or six square miles," he said. "One side, the west, is bounded by the Havel River, and the other two sides by the Eberswalde Forests. All four sides would be a cinch for them to guard. As I can't tunnel up through into the place, the best bet is to enter it from the only other way. I…."

"Land a plane?" Sir John gasped.

"No," Combat shook his head, "even though there is a nice little field there the Works' executives used to use for commuting purposes. No, to land a ship there would simply be asking for a Mauser rifle slug in my hide. Tell me, Sir John, are we still making propaganda leaflet flights over the Rhine?"

"Yes," the Cabinet member replied in a tired voice. "And I'm afraid it will be kept up until England runs short of paper and printer's ink. Perhaps, though, there'll be a Cabinet shake-up before then. However such flights are still being made."

"Then that's the answer," Combat said with a curt nod for emphasis. "From what I've learned Hitler doesn't care what we toss down on his boobs because he's got them too damn scared to read anything that hasn't got his fourth grade handwriting on it. Therefore, they don't pay much attention to the propaganda planes. That is, not unless they get close to some military concentration center."

"But the Breslau Works is…" Sir John started to say.

"Sure it is," Combat nodded. "But what I'm getting at is this. A leaflet flight wouldn't be bothered much if it headed for some remote spot in Germany. Also it would be flying at top ceiling. With that type of bomber you have darn near a gliding range clear to China from top ceiling. So, here's my suggestion. I'll take passage on a leaflet ship. At the right time my pilot will cut his engines and float down over the northern end of the Breslau Works. Then me and my parachute will bail out. I'll make it a free fall as long as I dare, then crack the silk. Meantime the plane will glide on as far as it can before the pilot has to open his engines and climb for altitude. Roughly, I'd say he'd be a good fifteen miles away by then, and the folks at the Works wouldn't even hear him."

"If only it could be done!" Sir John breathed as Combat finished. "But, there'd still be the task of getting out again… assuming you found my agent alive."

"I can take that up when I'm on location," the Yank born pilot grunted. "Tell me about this agent. I mean things that will help me to spot him… if he happens to be around to be spotted."

Instead of answering Sir John opened his desk drawer, thumbed about in it for a moment, then pulled out a photograph and silently handed it to Combat. The Yank found himself looking at a picture of a man about his own height. He was neither good looking nor bad looking. Oddly enough, though, the features were more Teutonic than English. The face was flat and full, the forehead was high, the eyes small and set wide apart, and the hair looked like clipped whiskbroom bristles.

Turning it over he read the printed description. The man's name was George Rollins. He was five foot eleven inches tall. He had blond hair and blue eyes. He had one gold tooth and a curve scar on his left elbow. And he had a service record that made Combat nod in frank admiration. His Intelligence number was 27.

"I hope he's alive," Combat said looking up at Sir John. "A lad with his record doesn't deserve to die for a long time."

"War doesn't pick favorites," the Cabinet Minister said grimly.

"There's two items not listed there. One is that he is an expert machinist. That's the work he was doing at the Breslau plant, last time he was able to contact me. And here's the other item. The way you will be able to convince him instantly that you come from me. It is a single word… Trafalgar. Each agent I send out has a secret identification word, known only to himself and me. I've told four men Rollins' word, and they are now dead. I pray to God that in telling you I am not making it five."

Combat laughed, but it was not a particularly cheerful laugh. "Check on that prayer," he said.

"When do you wish to start?"

Combat looked out the window and across the Thames to the London house tops on the other side. The shadows of night were beginning to settle down, and as though some great giant were drawing his hand over the city, the nightly blackout was beginning to take place. He shrugged and turned back to Sir John.

"I might just as well have tomorrow's breakfast at the Breslau Works."

CHAPTER 6
COMBAT TAKES OFF

NO MORE than a dozen lights glowed at one corner of the huge expanse that was Hendon Airdrome. Not because the commanding officer there was trying to save on Government electricity bills, but rather, because the drome was only a little over fifteen miles from the heart of London, and could serve as a perfect land mark for raiding enemy bombers aiming at the British capital. They had to be very careful.

The lights that were on, however, shed their rays on a scene of precision like activity. Five twin engined Vickers-Armstrong bombers were being made ready for a long range flight deep into the heart of German territory. The gunners were checking their aerial machine guns just in case trouble did come zooming up out of the darkness. Pilots were checking instruments and the hundred and one other things that fell under their charge. Mechanics were swarming over the ships like so many busy ants. And the navigators and bomb observers were helping with the loading of the empty bomb compartments.

Only it was not bombs they were loading inside. Instead it was bundle after bundle of printed leaflets that in another three hours would go fluttering down through the night to German soil to inform any reader that Hitler was a first class bum, and that the real German people were really right guys, and for heavens sake why do you fellows swallow all that verbal garbage that Adolf and his bums have thrown at you?

Standing with Combat was Sir John. He was not watching the leaflet loading, however. He was staring at Combat's face, feeling lower than a snake's belly, and wondering just how he could put the words he wanted to say into a sentence that didn't slobber over at the edges.

"If you want to change your mind, William," he began and stumbled on the rest. "I mean…."

"I understand, Sir John," Combat said, turning to him with a grin. "And thanks. I don't want to change my mind, however.

I... Well, let's say that I'm curious as hell to find out the truth about Rollins. But... don't expect me back until you see me, sir. There's no telling what whistle stops there may be on the way."

"Please God, you do return safely," Sir John murmured. Then with a sharp curse, "Damn my eyes, a fine chief of Intelligence I'm making of myself. Shouldn't have come out here if I can't show the guts you're showing, my boy. Your uncle would give me a fine lecture if he were here. Sorry, William."

Combat said nothing. He simply grasped the Cabinet member's hand and pressed hard. Then the pilot of one of the bombers came striding over. He had been taken into the secret, naturally, but he was the only pilot of the group who knew that he was going to dump something besides leaflets down on Germany. He saluted Sir Henry and grinned at Combat.

"Time for passengers to get aboard," he said. "Is your passport in good order, my man? Or don't you plan to come back?"

"I'll be back to get cockeyed at your wake, pal," Combat said and jabbed him in the ribs. "Sure you can get this crate off? Or should we send for a real pilot?"

"And prevent a perfectly good crack-up?" the other echoed in amazement. "A fine loyal subject of Adolf's you are! You come right along with me. You'll even sit beside me. I've often wanted to see what a chap looked like just before he crashed."

"Good Lord!" Sir John gasped weekly. "Are you two lads insane? You'd think...."

"Quite, Sir," the bomber pilot said and led the way over to his ship.

Sir John clicked his lips shut and wanted to kick himself for having opened them. He'd seen a lot of dangerous service in the last World War and knew perfectly well that men going into battle always made fun of the venture ahead. They kidded and horsed around with one another, if for no other reason than to damn well keep serious thoughts out of their heads. To think of dying is twice as agonizing as the real thing, they say.

As the pair started to climb into the plane, Sir John touched Combat on the shoulder and offered his hand.

"All the luck in the world, William," he said gravely. "I'll notify Wing Commander Nevens that you won't be back for a while. Have you any message?"

Combat gripped the other's hand and started to shake his head. He checked it and nodded instead.

"Yes, I have, Sir Henry," he said. "You might tell Colonel Nevens that I've gone to take lessons in keeping my fanciful imagination from going haywire. I believe he'll approve of that."

Before the startled-eyed Cabinet member could say anything, Combat climbed into the plane, pulled the door shut and went forward to take the seat next to the pilot's. The pilot, whose name was Bidford, was all airman, now. His eyes raced over the instrument panel to check and re-check everything. Then he slowly eased open the twin engines and trundled the big craft out onto the field and swung it around into the wind. There he waited until the other three were in position. Three minutes later, Hendon Airdrome fell away from the bomber's wheels and the plane went curving up and around into the night. At ten thousand feet it leveled off, heading east. The navigation officer handed Bidford his exact course. The pilot put the nose of the plane right in the groove, and relaxed a bit in the seat. "Well, you've got three hours to kill, Combat," he said. "Care to read some of the literature we're carrying?"

"Nix!" the Yank grunted. "I want to keep my dinner where it is."

"Of course I know where you're going," Bidford said, giving Combat a glance out the corner of his eye. "But that's all. Just what do you expect to do when you get there, eh?"

Combat stared out through the windshield at the blackness of night perpetually rushing toward them.

"I'd give a hell of a lot to know the answer to that, myself!" he murmured.

CHAPTER 7
COURAGE TAKES A DIVE

I T WAS just after one o'clock on the following morning as the four pamphlet-laden bombers cut through the air at twenty five thousand feet over the Elbe River. Their objective was the city of Brandenburg. There they would dump some of their load and then circle around toward the southwest, dropping more leaflets as they made their way back to a final landing on a French field behind the Maginot Line. Which, by the way, was one good thing about this leaflet-dropping business. You landed in France to join a real bombing squadron, instead of returning to England. It was sort of ferrying replacement planes to France by way of Berlin, you might say.

At the moment, however, Combat was not thinking of landing in France and becoming part of an active service bombing unit. Staring from the window of the darkened compartment he picked out clusters of lights here and there, and kept strict account of the towns they represented. If all went well, his bomber would leave the flight in another ten minutes and go sliding off more to the east. After five minutes in that direction Bidford would kill his engines, and the craft would start its long creeping glide toward the Breslau Works which was no more than a pin point on their maps right now.

If all went well? The thought raced through Combat's brain and made him mad. Why the hell shouldn't all go well? Save for a few searchlight beams, and some half-hearted archie fire to greet them as they slid in over the coast from the sea, the flight had been no more than a joy hop at midnight. He and Bidford had chewed the fat on a million things other than war, and it had all been very pleasant and swell. Now, though, as they were approaching the moment when they would quit the formation, they both had lapsed into silence, each more than content to mull over his own thoughts regarding the future.

Unconsciously Combat plucked at the material of the garments he was wearing. His regular uniform was back in England and he wondered when and if he'd put it on again. Naturally he couldn't go floating down into Germany as a British Air Force captain. And after considerable thought he had rejected Sir John's suggestion that he go garbed as a German officer. For no definite reason, he had had the feeling that a uniform of any nation was not the safest thing to be seen wearing around the Breslau Works. And so he had finally settled on the type of garb that seemed to fit best into the picture as he expected… and hoped… to find it. That was the greasy overalls, coarse shirt, jacket and cap of a German workman. A German who worked in a machine shop, to be exact. Rollins was supposed to be working at Breslau as a machinist, so it seemed the best bet to go dressed as one himself.

"It's been mostly guessing, pal," he murmured to himself. "But pretty soon you're going to see how close you came. And, Lady Luck, here's hoping you make it a bulls-eye score!"

Combat's thoughts were set asunder by the sudden sound of Archie guns bursting up at them from down below. He knew then, with sickening realization that their flight had been observed. And so did Pilot Bidford. They glanced at each other and frowned. Then Bidford cursed.

"Now just wouldn't the blighters wait until we're almost there!" he said in disgust. "Damn those archie gunners. They'll have lights on us in a minute, and maybe a flock of their single seaters will come up."

No sooner had Bidford spoken than long pencils of light sprang up from the ground far below and began swaying this way and that as their operators tried to pick up the invaders. Bidford glanced downward and bit off a sharp curse.

"Me, the fortune teller!" he snapped. "Just spotted a batch of exhaust flames. That means their night patrol single seaters are on their way up to find us. Want to go aft and have a go at one of the rear guns, eh? You might get in a lucky burst on one of the beggars. Never can tell, you know."

The urge within Bill Combat was great, but his sense of duty toward the bigger job at hand was even greater. He shook his head.

"Not tonight, Bidford," he said. "Nose her up and break away from the formation now. The other boys can have our share of the fun."

"*What?*" Bidford yelled. "You mean quit them? Leave them in the lurch? Hell, we can handle all the single seaters they want to toss at us with this type of ship. We'll just knock off a few of the beggars first and then go our merry way."

"Sorry, but it's no, Bidford," Combat said.

"Why the devil not?" the pilot demanded.

"Just playing it safe," Combat said and felt like a heel. "We might not be lucky, and we've got another job to do."

Bidford gave him a long hard stare. "I hope they give you a medal for it!" he grated.

CLICKING HIS teeth shut on that crack, Bidford pulled up and away from the three other planes. In less than no time they were seemingly alone in the clouds. Then suddenly they heard the faint yammer of machine gun fire in the air behind them. Impulsively, Combat glanced back out his window. A dozen searchlight beams were focussed on a patch of sky filled with twisting and turning planes. Combat could see the three bombers returning bullet for bullet that zipped out of the guns of half a dozen German single seaters that twisted and turned about the larger ships like so many angry wasps.

Fighting down the urge that was stronger than ever, Combat turned front and forced himself to forget the battle and concentrate on the course the ship was flying. There, some thirty miles

ahead, and some twenty seven thousand feet down, *should* be
the Breslau Works. In another fifteen minutes he would step
through the cranked open door of the bomber and go tumbling
head over heels down through space. In another fifteen minutes!
Bidford had already killed his engines and the big craft was
floating silently down through the night. The pilots' compartment door opened and the navigation officer stuck his head
inside. Bidford, however, didn't give the man a chance to open
his mouth.

"Never mind!" he barked angrily. "This is on special orders.
Special orders. Get back to your post!"

The navigator ducked back out of sight and Combat groaned
inwardly. He knew damn well the thoughts that Bidford was
thinking. The pilot was cursing him for making him quit the
fight several miles back there in the night sky. Bidford had
enlisted to drop bombs and fight, and he wasn't the kind of a
fellow who would leave the job to others. Yes, Combat knew
exactly how Bidford felt, and his heart sort of ached for the
youth. But, hell, there wasn't anything to be done about it. The
time to take chances would be when his feet touched the ground
about the Breslau Works. That was the job, and the only job.
Four men had tried it and died. What a fool the fifth would be
to risk his chances by taking part in an air scrap before he'd even
come within gun shot of his goal. Damn right! It was tough
on Bidford, and the plane's crew. But, hells bells, it was just as
tough on him.

"You better get set for your big adventure, Combat," Bidford's

A dozen searchlight beams were
focused on a patch of sky.

voice cut into his thoughts. "We're down to eleven thousand, now. I think that cluster ahead and to the right is the spot."

Combat fixed his eyes on the lights, picked up other groups of lights, and a river, too, and checked them all against the detailed strip map fastened to the instrument panel. Bidford was right. The pilot was going to hit his mark right on the nose. Pulling the seat pack 'chute straps up over his shoulders, Combat crossed them over and fastened the buckles. Then pulling a pair of goggles from his pocket he slipped them over his head and stood up.

"A fast return, Bidford," he said, and reached for the compartment door knob. "And happy landings, old man."

Bidford suddenly reached back, fumbled for Combat's hand and grasped it.

"Mind punching me on the snout before you leave, Combat?" he said, keeping his eyes fixed on the lights. "I was a bit of a selfish damn fool. I realize, of course, that this is the important thing."

"Forget it, kid," Combat chuckled. "I was just thinking of the boys in the other three bombers. Think how they'd have felt if we'd cleaned up that flock of Hun birds before they could even get in a shot. See you again, Bidford, and don't land in a Maginot tank trap. So long."

Giving the pilot a parting slap on the back, Combat stepped through the compartment door and made his way aft to the bomb compartment door. The members of the plane's crew stared at him wide-eyed as he turned the crank that pried open the door against the powerful slip-stream. However, they didn't ask questions. That wasn't part of their job, and besides they had seen this lad chumming around at Hendon with none other than His Nibs, the Right Hon. Sir John Baker.

BILL COMBAT

Once the door was cranked back enough to admit his body, Combat pulled the goggles down over his eyes, leaned out through the door opening and peered down at the ground. The cluster of lights was off to the right which meant that Bidford was gliding a hairline course that would take the ship over the extreme end of the enclosed area. A wind test made during the last five minutes of the glide had shown that the breeze was from the north. Therefore it would carry Combat to the south and away from the guards at the northern end, yet not too near the group of lighted buildings.

"At least, I hope it does!" Combat whispered to himself and swallowed hard. Some thirty five seconds later the plane was down as low as Bidford dared take it without being seen. That was a point some five thousand feet above the ground. The signal to Combat was a slight dipping of the right wing. When he felt the movement he knew the time had come. He stared down, and his imagination told him a thousand pairs of eyes were fixed upon him from the ground. "Colonel Nevens should read my thoughts right now!" he grunted. And with that, he dived out the door and into a great black emptiness.

CHAPTER 8
THE DEVIL'S DEN

THE HIGH command of German Intelligence, one Hermann Peiplow, paced restlessly up and down the length of his steel-walled room, located in the greystone building directly across the Wilhelmstrasse from the German Chancellery. At intervals he paused and swept his eyes over the panels of switches, dials, and countless other gadgets fitted to the steel walls. It was quite a room, that steel walled affair. Perhaps there was no other room in the world like it. At any rate, there undoubtedly wasn't any other room in the world that served such a purpose. Peiplow's special steel room was the nerve center of the Nazi system of ruthless war making. From that room Peiplow could contact any German ship, submarine, airplane, troop headquarters, or Nazi agent anywhere in the world. Through the use of a special secret radio detonating wave he could explode mines and ammo dumps a thousand miles away. On the second day of the war his hand, throwing a switch in that Berlin room, had destroyed a German cargo boat off the China coast as a British man-of-war came boiling up over the horizon to seize her and take her into Singapore.

Right at the moment, his hands twitched from fuming impatience. And he was just about mad enough to let go for a second and throw one of the switches and blow up something just by way of letting off steam and appeasing his eternal lust to destroy. For half an hour he had been waiting for the daily report from his head agent in London.

Suddenly he stopped pacing. A small blue light on one of the panels was blinking. He reached the panel in three long strides and flipped up a switch and put his lips to a small grilled opening in the wall.

"Well, speak up!" he snarled.

"Agent X-four-B is ready on wave length Sixty Seven, *Herr* Peiplow," a voice spoke out of the wall.

"About time!" Peiplow grated and moved over to an adjacent panel.

There he snapped on a couple of switches and twisted a few tuning knobs. By so doing he made contact with X4B of London on a special transmitting wave that no other station in the world could tap. Only the operator in the control room above could tune in on that wave length, and if he did so, Peiplow would hear a click, much the same as the click one hears on a party phone line. And if Peiplow should hear a click the man in the control room would die... and that man knew it absolutely.

"You're late, you dog!" Peiplow roared when he had made contact. "Thirty-seven minutes to be exact, and...."

"I know, *Herr* Peiplow," a slightly whining voice came out of the speaker. "But it was for the best of reasons. I have great news for you *Herr* Peiplow!"

"Well?" the man in Berlin snarled when the other did not

continue. "Is this to be one of those fool American games of questions and answers? Tell me what you have to say!"

"The man you want leaves London tonight," the agent said. "Not fifteen minutes ago he left the War Office with Sir John Baker. They are now on their way to Hendon Airdrome. He is to take part in a propaganda raid, but he will drop by parachute into Germany. I heard the entire conversation with my own ears. Evidently Sir John still doesn't realize there has been a dictograph in his office for weeks. He...."

"The devil with Sir John!" Peiplow snapped. "What about that swine, Combat? What part of Germany is he heading for? Where is he going to land?"

"The Breslau Works, *Herr* Peiplow," the agent said. "I... I believe he is going to attempt to contact another one of Sir John's agents."

"Why are you hesitating?" Peiplow roared and his eyes narrowed to slits. "Are you making up stories? By God, if you are...!"

"No, *Herr* Peiplow!" came the whining voice. "I... something went wrong with the dictograph for a little while, and I could not hear all of the conversation. But I do know he plans to parachute down into the Breslau Works. And I am sure he hopes to contact another agent."

"And you don't know who that agent is, eh?" Peiplow demanded.

"No, I do not," the agent replied with tears in his voice. "When I again made the connection they had stopped speaking of him. I am sorry *Herr*...."

"Hold your blabbing tongue!" Peiplow shouted. "Tell me this, if you can, you blundering fool. Have the British captured one of your agents in the last two days? I speak of Agent B-Seven-H."

"Yes, they have!" the other cried in surprise. "Not an hour after I delivered your sealed orders to him. I swear, *Herr* Peiplow, it was no fault of mine. I warned him to go into hiding as I knew the British suspected him, and…."

"Enough of your talk!" Peiplow cut him off sharply. "Get back to your work, and you had better not be late with your report again. I have plenty of men to take your place should you die suddenly. Remember that!"

WITH A snort Peiplow snapped up the switch and spun the dials back to their former positions. He did so with an angry gesture, but when he went over to his desk and jabbed one of a row of many inlaid signal buttons, his eyes were bright and his thick lips were twisted back in a gloating leer.

"Captain Combat!" he breathed. "Right into my little trap. *Gott*, I shall always remember this glorious day!"

A buzzer sounded, and an unseen voice inquired,

"*Ja, Herr* Peiplow?"

"Send for *Herr* Franz Khole!" Peiplow barked without turning around. "I wish to see him here at once."

"*Ja*, at once, *Herr* Peiplow," the unseen voice acknowledged, and there was the faint click of the inter-office phone circuit being broken.

The twisted leer still stamped on his face, Peiplow sat down at his desk, pulled a map toward him and bent over it intently. In less than five minutes a bell tinkled. Without taking his eyes from the map, the chief of German Intelligence reached out his hand and jabbed another button. The only door in the room swung open, and Franz Khole, head of the infamous Gestapo, Hitler's throat-cutting secret police, stepped into the room.

Khole was a big hulk of a man. He bulged in all directions, almost as much as Hitler's bed fellow, Goering. To a certain extent his face looked something like Peiplow's. It was flat, it had small black eyes, and thick lips. As a matter of fact if there were to be a contest to pick the most repulsive looking man in Germany, the judges would undoubtedly call it a draw between Khole and Peiplow. And they were alike in intellect, too. Either of them could conjure up the most god-awful ways to torture and kill innocent persons. But, of course, Hitler had taught them all he knew, and *Der Fuehrer* was admittedly tops in that department.

"I hope it is good news, *Herr* Peiplow," Khole said eagerly as he spread himself on a chair. "*Ach,* yes, it must be. You look very pleased, my friend."

"I am more than pleased," Peiplow nodded with a smile. "I think there is no greater sport than to set a trap for a two-legged swine, and then sit back and watch him step into it."

"You mean…?" Khole cried. Then began again. "You mean that this Combat is in your trap?"

"He will be before the dawn comes," Peiplow said. "I have heard from London. In a few hours Combat will be on his way to Germany. In a propaganda plane. He will parachute down into the Breslau Works."

"The Breslau Works?" gasped Khole. "Then that agent was caught, eh? The one with that message you sent him?"

"The same!" Peiplow chuckled. "And just as I planned. You know how thorough I am, my friend. Step by step I lay my traps, and my victim never escapes."

"Granted," Khole nodded with a slight frown. "Still I wonder."

"Wonder what?" Peiplow asked in an icy voice.

"How wise it is to let the British even suspect anything about the Breslau Works," Khole said slowly. "After all...."

"Bah!" Peiplow snorted. "You can't have the heart of a chicken in this game. Let them suspect. They'll never find out until it is too late. Besides I had a double reason for rousing their interest in the Breslau Works. And it appears that you have failed in your job, my dear Khole!"

The Gestapo head half rose from his chair, eyes blazing and face beet red. When he met the ice cube on either side of Peiplow's nose he sank back and growled in his throat.

"*Der Fuehrer* has made no complaints of my work!" he said.

"He would, if I were to tell him that there is an English agent already in Breslau," Peiplow barked at him.

"What? Impossible! It isn't true!"

"Combat is on his way to attempt to contact another British agent in Breslau!" Peiplow said evenly. "Of that I am positive, and...."

"But that can't be!" Khole cried. "Not even a fly could enter or leave that place without my knowing it!"

"That, my dear friend," murmured Peiplow, "is one of the many reasons why I sit here as chief of Intelligence, while you are only head of the Gestapo. Because I have the superior brain. Of course no one has entered or left the place since you took charge. But were there not workers *already* there? Yes, I know, you checked them all, carefully. But remember, my dear friend, though the British agents are swine, they are not all fools."

"Then you think…?" Khole gulped and stopped.

"I am positive!" Peiplow said bluntly. "So you see, I am really getting two birds with one stone. That dog, Combat, and the other who has been locked in Breslau unable to get out."

"Parachuting down into Breslau!" Khole breathed. *"Gott,* I am tempted to go there and fill him with rifle bullets, myself, as he floats down."

"And I would suggest to the Leader that you be shot for a fool!" Peiplow snapped. "No, Combat will not be killed so soon. We will give him plenty of rope. We will first let him contact this other agent, if he can. And then…."

THE CHIEF of German Intelligence stopped and laughed deep in his throat. The sound was like dishwater going down the drain.

"And then," he continued presently, "the great Captain Combat will answer to me, his master. He will tell me a lot of things. He will tell me about that new British bombing plane. He will tell me the strength of the British coast air defenses. He will tell me a lot of things. *Gott,* yes!"

"You think you can make him speak?" Khole asked in a voice quite indicative of how he felt on the subject.

"Most certainly I do!" Peiplow said.

"I wonder," Khole murmured. "You failed once… at Hamburg. He is a fool, and a swine, but he does not lack courage."

"I grant you that," Peiplow said with a smile. "But once he is in my trap, have no fear, my friend. I have a way to make the bravest man in the world spill out his inner most thoughts. And not even remember he has spoken them… if, and when, he returns to normal."

Heartless and utterly cruel minded though he was, Khole shivered slightly as he looked into Peiplow's eyes.

"Yes, of course you have," he said. "And I would not care to be in this Combat's shoes for all the riches and glory in the world. I still wonder a bit, however. Somehow it would please me more to see a hated enemy of mine return to live in disgrace among his own people. Why not let this Combat return with information that will cost even more British lives? Would that not give you greater satisfaction?"

"No!" Peiplow said viciously. "I have promised myself that with my own eyes I shall see his cursed blood soaking into the ground. If, as you so foolishly think, I do fail to make him speak, I shall still have his life. And after all, to make him speak is really not that important. *Der Fuehrer* has England's doom in the hollow of his hand."

"That is true," Khole murmured. "That is indeed true. When *Der Fuehrer* gives the signal… it will be the beginning of the end. The tests were a complete success."

"As I knew they would be," Peiplow said. "The Leader has the greatest brain on earth. He will never fail. And meantime, our swine enemies are very worried indeed. You and I have planted the seed deep. Yes, they wonder and worry a lot about our little secret of the Siegfried Line."

The two men looked at each other for a moment. Then each threw back his head and the steel walled room echoed and reechoed with booming, roaring laughter.

CHAPTER 9
THE SKY ROUTE TO HELL

FIVE THOUSAND feet. Four thousand. Three thousand! Bill Combat's body hurtled down through the darkness of night like a meteor in high gear. The wind whipped and lashed his plunging body, and his brain screamed for him to jerk the ring. But he refused to give in to the fear-tipped desire. He had carefully calculated the rate of his fall, and he was counting now.

At fifteen he would yank the ripcord ring and still have time for his 'chute silk to "catch" and check his swift, headlong rush.

"Fifteen!"

The word was loud in his brain but the wind whipped it away from his lips before it could reach his ears. Automatically his hand had pulled the rip-cord ring, and a couple of seconds later invisible hands seemed to reach down from Heaven, catch him under the arm pits and jerk him back up. Then he was dangling at the end of his shroud lines, less than fifteen hundred feet over the black carpet stretched out beneath him.

In the distance he could see the lights of the Breslau buildings, but directly below was a sea of ink.

"Thank God there's no church steeple under me," he muttered through clenched teeth. "But the top of a pine tree isn't going to be so damn pleasant. Hell, I wish I could use a flashlight and get a look at what's going to smack the seat of my pants."

Even if he had a flashlight, which he didn't, he knew perfectly well he would not have used it. Even a dumb German guard would wonder what a flashlight was doing floating around in the night air. No, his immediate fate was in the lap of the gods. In fact, the seat of his pants was in the lap of the gods. A few moments later it turned out that the gods were exceedingly kind.

Combat's feet hit soft ground. He instantly let his knees buckle and momentum let him down hard, but fortunately on soft ground.

Quickly twisting over, he stretched out flat and grabbed the shroud lines and jerked to spill the air from his 'chute before the ground wind caught it and started dragging him. Then, crawling forward on hands and knees, he gathered up the silk and got out of his harness.

For a few seconds he stood perfectly still, eyes peering into the darkness, ears strained for the sound of airplane engines. He saw nothing and heard nothing. He grinned thinly.

"Hope that scrap is still going, so you can have a crack, Bidford," he whispered.

Holding the 'chute silk and harness in his arms, he walked slowly toward his right. Darker shadows in that direction told him there were trees there, not over thirty feet away.

When he reached the trees he got down on all fours and slowly worked his way deep into the underbrush. There he dug a hole in the pine needles and soft earth and laid the parachute silk and harness to rest. Crawling back to his starting point, he stood up and took careful stock of his surroundings. As far as he could tell there were woods to his right and left, and behind him. Straight ahead, towards the south, there was more or less open ground, high in some spots and low in others. About three miles away he could see the glow from the buildings of the Works. It was like a beckoning finger, and impulsively he started moving forward. A picture of the lay-out of the buildings was firmly imprinted in his brain. He silently thanked God he'd had the good fortune to visit the place during peacetime, and therefore knew which was the tool and machine building.

It was one of the first on the right after entering the main gates. A long, one-story affair with more windows than roof. If Rollins was still alive the chances were that he would be working in the machine building. But if Rollins were not alive… Combat clamped his teeth down hard on the thought.

"Then you *will* have a job to do, pal," he said to himself. "You'll have to dig out what's what around here, and then take it on the lam. And by the way, pal, how about starting to figure right now just how in hell you're going to get out of this place… if you are that lucky?"

WITH A muttered curse he brushed the thought aside. He did so for two reasons, one of them being that now wasn't a good time to think such thoughts, and the other because he had suddenly walked over a rise of ground to find himself not fifty yards from several rows of low-roofed hutments. The living quarters of the hired help at the Breslau Works, no doubt.

And there was no doubt about it. Both men and women in working clothes were entering and leaving the buildings. And a moment later Combat heard a sound that gave his heart a twist. It was the plaintive wail of a hungry baby. A few seconds later a dozen other infants joined in the chorus, and Combat unconsciously clenched his fist in biting rage at Nazi methods.

"What a hell of a fine place for a youngster to grow up in!" he grated. "That louse, Hitler, probably plans to have them at a work bench by the time they're five."

Slowly fading off to the right to lose himself in the dark shadow of a nearby tree, Combat studied the lay-out before him and debated his next move. He could see the machine and tool building, about half a mile away. Every light in the place seemed to be on, and as he peered at it intently he fancied he could see the figures of men and women at the various pieces of machinery. From the hutments at the base of the rise of ground upon which he stood, a narrow street ran straight along past the buildings to the main gates. Even at a slow pace he could walk the distance in ten minutes. But to do so he would have to pass a hundred or more Germans dressed as himself. And—he first noticed them at that exact moment—several of the Works guards who strutted around in their pea-green uniforms and bell-hop hats.

"Not so good," he murmured with a scowl. "I might not be noticed, but then again I might."

He continued staring at the scene. A whistle mounted atop one of the nearer buildings let go with a shrill blast, and almost instantly he noted that the low-keyed hum of turning machinery slackened. The shift at one plant was obviously through, and the machinery had been shut down for a spell. Combat watched the file of workers coming out passing other workers going in, and told himself that his job was going to be even harder. The place was obviously working at full capacity, in shifts. His plan had been to get as close to the building as possible and watch those coming out, hoping and praying that Rollins would be one of them. But with the men working in shifts, he stood a fair chance of having to park near the entrance of that particular building for twenty hours or more.

"Still not so good!" he grunted. Then with a shrug, "But maybe you'll have to do it, kid. Anyway, for pete's sake, do *something!*"

He turned and moved to his right, his idea being to circle the group of hutments and approach the machine and tool building from the rear. That would take him twice as long as by the narrow street route, but for the present, time was not exactly the important thing.

Twice he had to freeze back into a building shadow and stand there holding his breath as a couple of workers strolled by. He cursed himself for his bad case of nerves. Sooner or later he'd have to let the workers see him. Somehow, though, he wanted to avoid that situation until he had definitely spotted the man he hunted.

"And that may be never!" he reminded himself grimly. "For all you know…" The rest of that thought was cut off short, for in turning a corner, he had come within a hair's breadth of slamming straight into a figure moving, head down, toward him. In the nick of time he leaped to one side, but perhaps it didn't matter. The advancing man looked up. Startled surprise lighted his eyes, then his face twisted in anger.

"What are you doing, sneaking around the back of this building?" the man barked harshly. "Stand where you are! The guard will...."

The mention of the word, guard, settled things in Combat's brain. Right or wrong, he had to shut the man up, and shut him up quick. And with that one thought in his brain, Combat dived forward, both hands outstretched.

CHAPTER 10
DEAD MEN CAN'T YELL

ONE HUNDRED and eighty-five pounds of solid bone and muscle hit that German amidships. A brick wall would have given ground under the impact and the man was no brick wall. So he went down hard on the flat of his back. But he was made of tough stuff, nevertheless. He wrenched savagely to one side and Combat almost went flying. But the Yank stayed put and jammed up both hands to lock his fingers about the man's neck and choke off the wild bellow of alarm that was on its way up the throat.

Putting every ounce of his strength into the effort of jamming his two thumbs deep into the leathery flesh, Combat was still unable to hold his man pinned. The German twisted and thrashed about like an angry cobra. Suddenly a hand jerked upward, and out the corner of his eye Combat saw the dull gleam of a Luger. His heart stopped beating and his ears seemed to ring already from the bark of the gun, although it had yet not been fired. A split second to grasp the danger, and then Combat was a whirlwind of furious action. He let go of the man's neck, smashed one fist up under the chin, twisted and crashed the other fist down on the Luger. There was the sharp snap of wrist bones  letting go, and a choked groan of pain spilled from the man's lips. Despite his broken hand he tried to twist over and bring the Luger into line with Combat's body. The twisting motion made it possible for Combat to brace himself. He drove upward with his clenched fist once more, and the blow knocked the German stone cold. In fact it did more than that. It broke his neck. Even as Combat dragged the limp body back into the shadows, the man was dead.

Panting and gasping for breath, Combat simply lay across the dead man for a moment, at least long enough for balls of colored light to stop dancing around in his brain. The dead German had not fired his Luger, but he had managed to do the next best thing just before Combat's fist had knocked the gun down. That was to lay the barrel of the Luger across Combat's temple, and not exactly "lay" it at that!

Presently the pain faded and left only an ache in Combat's head. He got up on his knees and looked around. To have a dead

German on his hands complicated matters. He couldn't leave him there to be found by a patrolling guard, and he certainly couldn't take the man along with him. There was only one answer to his problem. The German's body had to be towed away where it wouldn't be found for some time, at least.

As though the gods still felt playfully kind, Combat's eyes suddenly lighted on a huge box pushed up against the rear of the building against which he crouched. He got slowly to his feet and went over and lifted the cover. He put in his hand and felt gobs of oil-soaked waste, and felt very happy indeed. It was undoubtedly a receptacle for machine waste and shavings. Holes had been bored in the sides to let in plenty of air, to prevent spontaneous combustion.

"Not good, but it'll do," Combat muttered and went back to the dead German.

A moment or so later, as he was stuffing the German down under the piles of waste, he suddenly halted his actions. His hand felt a flat bulge in one of the pockets. He took out the bulge and found it to be the man's wallet. Stuffing it in his own pocket for the time being, he completed his job and lowered the lid of the box. Returning to the scene of the battle he scooped up the Luger and slipped that into his pocket. Then, as though walking on eggs, he continued on his way toward a vantage point that afforded him a good look at the front of the machine and tool building.

IT WAS a clump of shrubs not fifty feet from the entrance. By squatting down behind them he could see anyone who entered the building and get a good look at the person's face as he passed under the door light. For an hour he sat hunched behind those shrubs, and at the end of that hour he knew beyond all possible doubt that the hope of maintaining a twenty hour vigil was completely out of the picture. Hot needles were already beginning to prick his cramped muscles. And, besides, once dawn came, he'd look funny as hell crouched behind that clump of shrubs, for almost any passerby would be able to see him.

"Unless there's a change of shifts before dawn, and you spot Rollins," he muttered to himself, "you're going to have to stick your neck out into full view. And maybe have it catch what you gave to that dumb Hun."

As he thought of the dead German he suddenly thought of the wallet in his pocket. If for no other reason than to kill time, he took it out and started to thumb through its contents. The first card he pulled out stated that the man's name was Wilentz, and that he was a civilian police deputy at the Works and could be called upon at any time to assist the guards in any manner the Guard commander saw fit.

The card explained a lot to Combat. He had wondered why the German, who had been wearing workman's clothes, had barked his questions and tried to act the typical Prussian officer of old. The card explained it, and Combat felt a little bit better for having been forced to kill the man. It was simply the Nazi system on a small scale. Wilentz had been no more than a spy working at the plant to keep his eyes and ears open for any bit of unrest or dissension among the hired help. He would report the "guilty" ones to his superiors, and in due course they would be facing the rifles of a firing squad.

Sticking the card back, Combat pulled out another one and glanced at it—and almost let out a yell of joy. It was Wilentz's identity and time card for the *machine and tool building!* Hardly able to believe his eyes, Combat stared at the card. It gave the workman's name, the shift he worked, his locker number in the plant, the number of his machine, and the type of work he was doing.

That card removed Combat's greatest stumbling block in the path of his entrance into the building… a wild hope that had been fermenting in his brain during his vigil behind the shrub clump. A wild hope that had gradually been killed off as he had noticed that every man who entered the building showed some kind of a card to the uniformed guard who stood just inside the door.

"It was one of these cards!" he whispered excitedly. "Lady Luck, is this the break of breaks. The lug worked the two A.M. to noon shift. It means that in just fifteen minutes he'd be going through that door. Only *I'm* going through instead."

THE NEXT fifteen minutes seemed like fifteen hours to Combat. A million and one wild, crazy hopes flashed through his brain; a million and one firecracker thoughts. A million and one tremors of dread and foreboding. What would he do once he was inside? What would he see? Rollins? Suppose Rollins didn't work that shift? After all, his luck was taking a fast and furious ride. Things were breaking too good for him.

"So what?" he told himself harshly. "You've got to keep on riding your luck, pal. Maybe you won't find Rollins this trip. Hell, maybe he isn't around to be found. But here at the Breslau

Works monkey business is going on, part of it in that building right over there. So you're going in for a look. You're...."

A whistle atop the building tooted to high heaven and instantly the roar of machinery within the building was stilled. As though by magic, a couple of hundred men in working clothes gathered in front of the place and formed a line. The doors were thrown open and two guards appeared to take up positions on opposite sides of the open doorway. One started looking at the cards of the men filing out, and the other looked at the cards of the men coming in.

For a second Combat hesitated. Here were two shifts. A perfect chance for him to get a look at the faces of at least four hundred men who worked in the building. Should he stay where he was and have that look? Or should he take advantage of the opportunity actually to get inside the place? His thoughts waged battle against one another and five seconds ticked by, then he made up his mind.

"If Rollins *is* dead," he muttered. "I'd have to wait until this shift came around again. A good twenty-four hours. Nix! It's inside for you, Combat, and keep your fingers crossed, pal!"

He eased out from behind the clump of bushes, shuffled over to the ingoing line and took his place.

CHAPTER 11
TRAFALGAR!

"YOUR CARD, you! Hold it up, you fool!"

The guard's harsh voice cracked against Combat's ears. He mumbled an apology and held his card higher. The guard took a look, and Combat's heart seemed to skip a beat. It seemed a year before the guard grunted and gave him a push that sent him farther into the building. Swallowing hard with relief at having successfully passed the barrier, Combat joined the others trooping into a huge room completely lined with lockers. Wilentz's locker was No. 298 but Combat did not go straight toward it, once he had found it in the row. He didn't because workmen were hanging up their jackets and caps in the lockers on either side.

For the first time, Combat realized that Wilentz was undoubtedly known to the men who shared lockers with him, and perhaps to a hundred or more of the men in that room. A cold sweat broke out on his chest, and he bent down to fumble with his shoelace to kill time and give the men near his locker a chance to hang up their things and move to the working room.

Finally there was no one near locker No. 298, and he hurried over, stuck his jacket inside, and went on into the work room himself. From one end to the other it was filled with machines of practically every description. Combat's eyes eagerly sought for signs that would give him a clue as to what the place was turning out. But right then and there he ran smack up against the wall of complete disappointment. There were brass, nickel, and steel parts all over the place. Lengths of pipe, pieces shaped like angle irons, others that could be piston rings or engine valves, or most anything else small and made of metal. With a sinking heart he realized that the place could be turning out almost anything… and probably was. At no place in the great room did there seem to be the finished product of all those machines.

That fact, however, raised his hopes a bit. He shouldn't have expected to see the finished article—not if it was some great military secret. The Nazis were not alone in that practice. Lots of nations followed it. Take the Liberty engine of the first World War, for an example. It was made in five different factories, and assembled in a sixth. Thus not a single workman knew what the whole was like.

"Well, are you going to your machine? Or should I get you a chair so that you can sit down and rest?"

The barking voice in Combat's ear almost made him jump out of his working clothes. He gulped, swallowed, stole a hasty glance at the glaring eyes of a guard standing at his elbow, and then went shuffling over toward the row of drill presses set against the right wall, because the card in his pocket said that Wilentz worked on drill press No. 8, drilling bolt holes in brass pipe clamps.

THREE MINUTES later he was hard at work at drill press No. 8, keeping his head bent and thanking his lucky stars that during his general mechanical education he had received enough instruction in the operation of a drill press to know how to run one. To his right was a box holding at least a thousand of the small pipe clamps. He would pick one up, slip it into the form jig, and screw it up tight. Then, sliding it under the vertical drill, he would start the drill motor with the foot pedal. Then, grasping the drill handle, he would lower the spinning drill down into the jig guide hole. Continued pressure on the drill handle would force the drill to chew its hole through the brass. Too much pressure and the drill would clog, spin the jig out of his grasp and whirl it around to give his fingertips a nasty crack. Too little pressure and the drill would give forth a high whining note, and the singular smell of heated lubricating oil.

When the holes were drilled he would remove the clamp, toss it into the box on his left, and take a fresh one from the box on his right. The same movements over and over again, until he longed to grab up a sledgehammer and sail into the machine. But naturally he didn't do that. In fact, the longer he stayed at the machine the more careful he became. Though he didn't turn his head, he had the feeling that eyes were watching him every now and then. His only hope for the present was not to attract any attention. And a drill snapping from too much pressure on the handle would get him plenty of attention. He would have to stop his machine, take out the stub and go to the stockroom for a new drill. And even in a civilian factory during peacetime, somebody always wants to know why, and how the hell the drill broke. He must be exceedingly careful.

At the end of two hours, when his eyes ached right through to the back of his head from constant concentration, he relaxed a bit and started looking around. A couple of workers nearby happened to look up at the same time, and the sympathetic smiles they gave him made Combat heave a great inward sigh of relief. His fellow workmen apparently took him for a new man on the job, trying to put up a good showing on his first night. And that made a hell of a big difference. That he worked Wilentz's machine seemed to be nothing unusual. As he gave thanks for that small crumb of comfort, the man working the machine next on his left looked up and confirmed it with words.

"A new hand, eh?" he muttered and spattered the floor at his feet with a stream of tobacco juice. "Thought there'd be one soon. We all knew the one who had your machine was one of the police deputies. Had it stamped all over him, the swine. He...."

The man stopped short, and sudden fear leaped into his watery eyes. Combat took a wild guess at the truth, laughed shortly, and shook his head.

"Let your tongue wag all it wants, my friend," he said in German. "I'm not one of those dogs. Not me!"

The German looked relieved, but he said no more and returned to his work. Combat was about to do so himself, when suddenly every fiber of his entire being seemed to become aflame, and his heart leaped up to choke his throat.

Not five drill presses away stood the man he sought.

For a couple of tingling seconds he tried to force himself to believe his eyes were playing tricks... that his imagination was truly going haywire, just as Wing Commander Nevens had warned him.

The man's looks fitted those of Rollins to a T. The height was a good five-seven, the hair was blond, and the eyes were blue. At that moment the man took something from his mouth and threw it onto the floor. A chew of tobacco, no doubt, but Combat didn't even give it a guess. A gold tooth flashed in the glow of the light over the man's machine. And then, as the man turned and bent over to pick up a new casting to be drilled, his left elbow came squarely into the rays of the machine light. Even from the distance of at least thirty-five feet Combat could see the two inch scar, a curving white line stamped on the darker skin of the elbow.

With more will power than he believed he possessed, Combat turned back to his own machine. Inwardly he trembled, and his mouth went dry as a bone from the excitement. He picked up a fresh pipe clamp to be drilled and it slipped from his fingers to clatter down onto the drill shelf. He cursed softly, steadied his fingers, picked up the clamp again and went to work.

Rollins is alive! Rollins is alive!

LIKE THE clanging of fire bells, that single statement of concrete fact pounded and pounded through Combat's brain. If paying attention to his job had been tough before, it was thricely tough now. He was virtually on fire with the wild desire to slip down to Rollins' machine and murmur the single word that would dispell the very last doubt—if there was one. The word Sir John had told him—*Trafalgar!*

However, he beat back the urge. He dared not leave his machine, for the very plain reason that no one else seemed to be quitting. Obviously they were there for one purpose only. To turn out as much work as possible, and no kidding about it. In time, though, he knew he would get a break. He'd just *have* to get a break. When Rollins went to the washroom, perhaps. Or maybe when....

He skipped the last bit of speculation because the opportunity he wanted was being dropped right into his lap. Rollins had stopped work at his machine and was moving his way, asking something of the man at each drill press. They all shook their heads and shrugged, and finally Rollins was at Combat's machine. Blue eyes looked into his, but there was nothing but a great weariness in their depths—the same look that he had seen in the eyes of all the other workers in the room. Soul and brain and body weariness from constant labor at high speed.

"Got a three-eights set screw for my jig?" Rollins asked in a low voice. "Mine snapped off, and the fellow in the stockroom here is a swine. You're new, eh? Well, I'll do the same for you some day. Look in your spare parts box, will you?"

Forcing a disgruntled look on his face, Combat grunted and pulled out his spare parts box. He bent over as he fingered through it so that Rollins would have to bend his head close to help him look.

When their heads were together Combat put his fingers on the desired set screw in the box and held it there.

"Don't know if I have one," he growled. "Yes, I'm new here. My name is… *Trafalgar!*"

As the word left Combat's lips the whole world seemed to stand still. If a gun had been shot off close to his ear it is doubtful that he would have noticed it. Every part of him was at hair-trigger tension, concentrated upon Rollins' reaction to the word. He thought he felt the man shiver slightly, then came the whispered words. Words whispered so softly he could hardly hear them. Words whispered in *English!*

"Dear God, it can't be!"

"It *is*, Rollins!" Combat whispered back. "I was with Sir John six hours ago. When and where can we talk?"

The British Intelligence man didn't answer for a moment. He bent closer to the box and poked around with his own finger. The finger was trembling like the prong of a tuning fork. Then presently he spoke again.

"Not in here, anyway," he said. "When the shift is over go to the workmen's canteen on the other side of the street. We are allowed an hour for our beer before we have to go to our hutments. Wait for me there. And for God's sake be careful! The beggars don't ask questions here. They just shoot!"

Rollins picked up the set screw he wanted, moved a step away from Combat and studied it under the machine light. He grunted and gave the Yank a smile of thanks.

"It will fit," he muttered. "You have saved me trouble, my friend, I will not forget. After the shift I will buy you a beer, yes."

With a nod the man shuffled back to his machine. Combat flashed a quick glance about the place, saw several workmen smiling at him. That meant they accepted him as one of them. He had helped a working friend.

He turned back to his own drill press, but the damn thing seemed to swim around before his eyes for a moment or so. He was on pins and needles with suppressed excitement, and his head felt light enough to float away from his shoulders. In another eight hours he would hear what Rollins had to tell him! In another eight hours he would learn the secret so closely guarded at Breslau. The answer to the mysterious concentration of German troops in the Siegfried Line!

In another eight hours....

CHAPTER 12
COMPANION IN HELL

WITH SLOW, almost deliberate movements, Combat crossed the canteen room with his mug of beer and slouched down at a small unoccupied table in the corner. The eight hours had finally passed on into history, and in addition to his weariness from the constant high speed work, he felt like a limp dishrag from the ever-mounting nervous tension from waiting... waiting... waiting for the hands of that big clock in the workroom to move around and around the face of the dial.

But that was all over, now. He was here in the canteen waiting for Rollins to join him. The British agent had grunted his thanks again in the locker room after the shift was through, but that was all. The man had immediately taken his things and gone out. When Combat left, his heart had skipped another beat as the door guard glanced at his card. For one hellish second he felt sure that he had been trapped—that the guard knew he was not Wilentz. But evidently the German simply enjoyed delaying a tired workman in getting to his beer, for he had presently been pushed on his way.

Elbows on the table and his body slouched over, Combat sipped his beer and let his eyes roam about the canteen room. He wanted to keep his eyes fixed on the door for the first sign of Rollins, but he refused to permit himself to do that. Better to take a drowsy interest in everything and let it go at that. Rollins would find him when he came.

When he came, or *if* he came?

The thought forced itself through Combat's brain and its significance sent a little chill down his spine. Supposing Rollins didn't show up? Supposing…?

He gripped the beer mug handle hard and gritted his teeth.

"Cut it, you sap!" he grated at himself. "Why shouldn't he show up? Why the hell shouldn't he?"

He could think of no reason why Rollins shouldn't show up, but that didn't help his state of nervousness even a little bit as the minutes dragged by to total up ten, then fifteen. His mug was empty. A couple of drill press operators grinned at him from another table, and sudden fear gripped him that they would invite him over, or perhaps join him at his own table.

To forestall that, he got up and took his mug over to the bar for a refill. He was about to toss a coin on the bar when a hand took hold of his arm and checked him.

"Let me buy this one, my friend. Didn't I promise to?"

Combat could have swung around and kissed Rollins out of sheer relief. Instead he grinned and nodded his head.

"That's right," he said with a grin. "But I buy us both one next time."

"As you wish," Rollins grunted, and pushed Combat's full mug his way.

Then, taking up his own and blowing off a bit of suds, he led the way back to the table where Combat had been sitting. For a moment they gulped at their drinks, then Rollins rubbed the back of his hand across his lips. In a moment he spoke.

"Sorry I'm late," he murmured. "Guessed you had no place to sleep. Arranged for you to bunk in the hutment where I am. What name are you using, and for God's sake how did you get past the door guard?"

Under the cover of taking a drink, Combat quickly described his arrival and the succeeding events. Rollins seemed to pale slightly and a baffled look seeped into his tired eyes.

"Wilentz's card?" he breathed. "That snake? But then, perhaps the guard didn't bother to read the name. They seldom do. I think you could flash any kind of a card on those stupid asses, and it wouldn't make any difference."

Rollins plucked at a hangnail on the middle finger of his left hand as he talked. When he finished he bit it off. He kept on biting the nail right down to the quick until Combat expected to see the blood spurt. But Rollins' teeth seemed to know when to stop. It became more the nervous gesture of a thoroughly exhausted man. Combat waited a moment for Rollins to say more, and when nothing was forthcoming he could hold back his questions no longer.

"What is going on here?" he murmured. "What are we making there in the shop? What have you found out?"

The British Intelligence man ran a tongue over his lower lip and then bent his head to the beer mug.

"A LOT—AND nothing," was his astounding statement. "Up to a month ago the place was turning out poison gas shells, flame throwing equipment, and so forth. But a month ago all that work was stopped. The whole place was turned upside down and we all became prisoners, more or less. In the machinery and tool building we were given work that could be used for almost any purpose. But little by little I was able to piece it together. We are making parts that go together to make some kind of a machine to be fitted on an airplane. No, not engines, or bomb sights, or anything like that. Something absolutely new. Something... I haven't the faintest idea what."

The man paused for a pull at his beer. Combat was about to speak, but when he saw that Rollins was going to continue he checked his words.

"I've tried every way to find out, but failed," he said bitterly. "But I'm sure it has a direct connection with the chemical division here. I made some tank valves a week or so ago, and they were shipped across the yard to the chemical division. Then the next day a plane was landed here on the field. We were all ordered to our hutments and warned not to look out the windows. We stayed there for over twelve hours. I took a chance and got one quick peak out my window. I could see one corner of the field. The plane was there, and so were the big shots of this place. They seemed to be fitting something under the fuselage. When it finally took off, I could see nothing. And next day changes were made in our work specifications. Parts I had turned out were given back to me to be changed. They had a funny smell about them. Like... well, like tomatoes that had been out in the sun too damn long. They... Drink your beer and tell me about your childhood!"

Rollins hissed the last and buried his face in his mug. For a second Combat was completely behind the eight ball, then out the corner of his eye he saw movement over by the canteen door. The guard commander and one of his flunkies had entered. The pair stared about the room, went over to the bar and swilled down a beer apiece. Then the senior officer glared around again and grunted.

"All of you be out of here in twenty minutes!" he boomed, and pointed a thick stubby finger at the large wall clock.

And with that he stalked out, his flunky tagging along at his heels. The sigh of relief that went up from the hundred or more men in the room sounded like the wind in the pine trees.

"There's one louse I hope to have the pleasure of killing before my time comes!" Rollins grated softly. "To say he is a skunk is to compliment the man. God, how they all hate him here. Talk about a disciplinarian! Look sideways at him and he'll give you a bullet between the eyes."

"To hell with him!" Combat muttered anxiously. "Tell me… the plane you saw landing here. Was it a Henschel high wing parasol type?"

Rollins' eyes widened in mild surprise.

"Why, yes!" he breathed. "Did you guess that, or did you know?"

Combat didn't answer for a moment. His mind was racing back to his eerie experience far out over the rolling waters of the North Sea. He pictured again that mysterious Henschel that swooped down low over the British tramp steamer, and of the strange, blood chilling fate which had befallen the boat. He hesitated, then in as few words as possible he told Rollins of his experience. When he had finished the agent was visibly trembling with excitement, though trying desperately to quell his body tremors.

"Good God, how can a plane destroy a ship at sea like that?" he gasped. "*If* it did. But what you tell me checks with two other things. I overheard the shop foreman talking with that louse, the guard commander. They said something about some tests being a success, and that Hitler saw them, himself."

"When did you hear this?" Combat couldn't get the question off his lips fast enough.

"Why, it was this evening," Rollins said. "Just before our shift went to work. I... Good God in Heaven! *That Dutch airliner you saw! He must have been—*"

"Right!" Combat groaned heavily. "No doubt about it. The one man in this world I want most to kill... right there for the killing. And I never dreamed...!"

Combat couldn't go on. The bitterness of a golden opportunity lost, perhaps forever, rose up within him to flood his brain with liquid fire. In a moment, though, he beat down his bitter thoughts and concentrated on the situation at hand.

"The other item?" he grunted.

"It may mean a lot, or nothing," Rollins said with a frown. "Two days ago they took some of us off the machines and put us to packing parts in boxes. I heard the rumor that everything was being shipped to an assembly point at Kleve."

"Kleve?" Combat echoed. "Are you sure? Kleve is no more than fifteen miles from the Holland frontier."

"I know," Rollins nodded. "I thought of that, so I did what

little checking I could. I mean, I sneaked into the shipping room… the stuff was taken away by train. Five hundred cases at least. And each one marked Commanding Officer, Base Twelve, Kleve."

COMBAT DIDN'T say anything. He slowly sipped his beer and looked blank and tired. His brain, however, was spinning over with hundreds of thoughts. He checked and rechecked a dozen things that had happened, and cudgeled his brain for answers that wouldn't stay put when he tried to tab them. And then, little by little, a faint glow of light came into being. A faint glow of the light of understanding, of deduction—or maybe just a wild, crazy hunch. Yet the more he concentrated on it, the brighter the light glowed.

"It can't be, and yet it might be," he argued with himself. "The Germans are bums, but not too stupid. Yeah, it's a fair bet that maybe they are planning to…."

He let the rest slide, almost not daring to think about it, and turned to Rollins.

"What else have you found?" he asked softly.

The Intelligence man looked unhappy and sighed into his beer.

"That's about all," he said. "I've been trying to get into the chemical division here, and find out just why the stuff we make is sent over, but so far I've failed. In case you don't know it, each separate group of workers here is a unit of its own. If you are found talking with men other than those in your shift you can kiss your life goodbye. And if you are caught talking with a man

from the forges, or the paint shops, or the chemical plants...
you'd get worse than death. However, I have hopes...."

The man finished with a half-hearted shrug and would have
lapsed into silence if Combat had let him.

"Meaning what?" the Yank pressed eagerly.

"Tomorrow is Thursday," Rollins said. "For some reason
the chemical plant only operates for a half day on Thursdays. I
believe the other half is given over to the big Nazis in the War
Research Bureau. They fly up from Berlin and spend all after-
noon in the plant. Anyway, for an hour at noon when there is
only a guard at the plant. I've worked out a way to slip over there
and get inside. I'm going to try it tomorrow."

The British Intelligence man paused again and a crooked
smile twisted his lips.

"Perhaps it is a blessing that you're here," he murmured.
"Though God knows I can't see how either of us can possibly
get out with our lives... even if I do discover something important tomorrow. However, with you here it doubles the chances."

"How about my joining you on your little visit," Combat
grunted. "That would double our success chances, too."

"No!" Rollins said sharply, and nibbled at his fingernail some
more. "It would mean certain death for both of us. Only one man
can try it, and as I've figured out a way, I'm the one to attempt it,
naturally. If I fail... well, then it'll be your turn. But...."

A bell clanged somewhere in the room, and all of the canteen's
occupants immediately got up on their feet.

"We part now," Rollins whispered. "To be too chummy will
arouse the guards' suspicion at once. This place is stricter than

a prison yard during the recreation period. Follow me to my bunk-house. Your cot is the last one in the left row. Go to it as though you knew it all the time. Don't come near me any more until tomorrow night after the shift. If I'm lucky, I'll tell you all about my little visit. Then we can plan. Good night, old man, and thank God for what's happened so far."

With a faint nod, Rollins walked over to the bar put his mug on it, then shuffled toward the door. Combat followed suit, and a few minutes later he was one of the two hundred who trooped into the bunkhouse. He saw that Rollins had a cot halfway along the row that backed against the right wall. He didn't look at Rollins. Like a German too damn tired to give even Hitler a tumble, he stumbled to the empty cot at the far end, peeled off his work clothes, and climbed under the coarse and not too warm blankets.

Five minutes later a guard stepped in, swept the place with his cold gaze, then flipped a switch. Darkness instantly filled the room. Presently, when Combat's eyes became refocussed to the sudden change, the darkness abated slightly. Through the row of windows opposite the foot of his cot he could see the first faint streaks of a new dawn.

A new dawn… of what? Life and hope? Failure and death? He wondered, and as he wondered the familiar eerie sensation crept up the back of his neck. He shivered a bit and clenched his teeth.

A new dawn was coming to that part of the world, but he would have to walk hand in hand with instant death before he would be able to talk with Rollins again.

And when he did, what would happen? On that unanswerable question his exhausted mind and body threw in the towel, and he dropped off the precipice of consciousness into a troubled and nightmare-filled sleep.

CHAPTER 13
NO MAN LIVES FOREVER

FEELING LIKE a man who has just lived through a twenty-four hour reprieve from the electric chair, Combat once again seated himself at a table in the workmen's canteen and forced some more vile-tasting beer down his throat. Every minute since he had awakened in the bunkhouse had been as an hour in the very depths of Hell. Every move he made, and every step he took, might have been his last one on this earth.

It had been all very well for Rollins to have told him to meet him again at the canteen, but Rollins was established at Breslau. The damn *Kommandant* of the place could have stopped Rollins and questioned him, and the Intelligence man would know all the answers. But his own case was different. He didn't know his way around, and ten million times during the passing of the agonizing hours he bitterly cursed himself for agreeing to meet the British Intelligence man again. Perhaps every minute he waited, keeping to himself, talking to no one, and above all avoiding every guard, was a minute, a precious minute completely wasted. What if Rollins didn't get into the chemical plant? What if he was caught and shot? And what if he did get in and discovered nothing of useful value? What if…? Twenty-four precious hours lost!

Damn it, to hell with Breslau! Hadn't he learned enough? Didn't it follow that Kleve on the Dutch frontier was the next door to be unlocked and opened? Yes. A thousand times, yes! He should take a chance. He was a fool to just sit and wait. It was damn stupid….

"Yeah, but here I am!" he muttered grimly, and wiped sweat from his forehead. "Here I am, but hell, if Rollins had only given me some kind of a high sign in the shop tonight! Just a look to let me know how he made out."

But during those ten grueling hours in the shop the British agent hadn't given him a glance of any description. He had stuck close to his bench, head bent and intent on his work. And he had seemingly purposely avoided Combat in the locker room. Something else, too, had worried Combat as he sat sipping the slop they served him for beer. While he worked at his drill press he had studied Rollins out the corner of his eye. The man looked different. Older, that was it! Sort of like a man who had walked to the edge of the grave and just barely stepped back in time. His face was duller in color, and his eyes held an even more listless look that gave them a different color, too. And….

"Cut it!" he rasped at his uncoiling brain nerves. "Perhaps he found out plenty and that's why he looked like the fag end of a hurricane. Maybe you'd look worse, pal."

He choked off his thoughts and again buried his face in the mug. When he came up for air he saw Rollins walking toward him. His heart started to hammer against his ribs in wild anticipation, and it was with a great effort he refrained from rising from his chair to meet the man. He held himself in check, however, and simply gestured to the chair placed next to his.

"Sit down, friend", he mumbled. "I was waiting to pay for your beer, but you were late. And now I see you have one."

"Such as it is," the other growled. He dropped into the chair and sat rubbing his hands over his face.

Combat waited until he could stand the silence no longer.

"Did you get in the chemical plant?" he whispered from behind his raised mug.

"Yes,"—came the muffled reply. "I've a lot to tell you, but first there are some things I must know. I have been here a long time and you are the only contact I have made. Your answers may help... help with our plan."

Combat wanted to swear aloud. What damn questions could he answer that would be more important than the discovery Rollins had made in the chemical plant? He got control of himself, however. Some agents work differently than others. Besides, Rollins' record was proof positive he knew the score most of the time. So he leaned slightly toward the man.

"Answers to what?" he breathed.

"Our forces in the Maginot Line," the other whispered. "What's their strength, and how close are they to the Belgian frontier?"

"Close to half a million, I believe," Combat answered. "And they are stationed practically at the Belgian frontier. In case Hitler tears up another scrap of paper and attacks... God, have you found it out, Rollins? *Is* Hitler going through Belgium to flank the Maginot Line?"

"Not sure, yet," came the reply from behind the face-pawing hands. "But about our fleet. Is there much of it in the Mediterranean?"

"I don't know for sure," Combat grunted. "I think...."

HAD A knife slashed all the way through his throat at that moment it could not have cut off his voice any quicker. He suddenly felt as though the whole world had dropped away from beneath his feet to leave him suspended motionless in a world of whirling red mist. His heart was ice in his chest, and his blood icewater in his veins. And he would not have been at all surprised if the hair on his head was standing straight up on end. In fact, he wouldn't have been at all surprised at anything else at that exact moment... *because there was a perfectly good fingernail on the middle finger of the left hand of the man seated next to him!*

He was trapped! He was caught cold! Satan, and the gods of war and death, were screaming with laughter at him because he was trapped; he was a doomed man and none knew it better than they. At lightning speed his brain raced back over the hours. Not a soul near the spot where he had landed; the shop guards seeming to hesitate when he showed his identity card; no one saying a thing to him; not a man asking where Wilentz had gone; last night that guard commander and his flunkey coming in for a look around the canteen. And a hundred and one other little things that all fitted together into a net that was now spread over him.

Rollins! He had been caught? He was dead? The very fact that

Rollins had not paid any attention to him in the shop meant that Rollins was dead. Because that man in the shop *had not been Rollins.* He had been this man, who sat rubbing his face there beside him. A double. A damn good double, complete even to the fake gold tooth. Of course they had not known about the real Rollins chewing his fingernail. They had....

Thoughts... thoughts... thoughts! They burned and slashed through Combat's brain during the split second he hesitated. The rats had known of his coming all along. They'd known him all along, given him rope, and were now trying to pump him before they fired the death bullet. Known about him all along... and left him alone. Why? That was easy to guess. To see if he would do exactly what he had done... *contact another British agent at Breslau.* He'd done that, and... killed Rollins just as surely as if he had put a gun to the man's temple and pulled the trigger.

White flames of blazing rage leaped high within Combat. For one tiny moment of berserk insanity he was tempted to throttle the life out of the rat there at his side. And he could do it before anybody in the room could make a move to prevent it. However, he beat down that savage, furious desire. To kill now would be to take his own life, and for no damn good reason save burning revenge.

No, there was part of the game still to be played. The Germans held a fistful of aces against the mess of porridge the Devil had dealt him. But he had one last play left... bluff. So long as this damn German didn't know he'd been unmasked he'd keep

Out of nowhere, a gun appeared in his hand.

pumping for information. Okay, he'd get information. And maybe he'd get....

"Let's see," Combat murmured. "I think Sir John told me that three squadrons of line ships had been sent out to join the torpedo squadron that went there two weeks ago. But, why do you ask, Rollins? Has all this something to do with what you found out today?"

"A lot," came the answer from the face buried in the beer mug. "I'll tell you all about it in a minute. First, though, the Canadian troops. Have any arrived, yet?"

Combat's right hand under the table clenched into a rock hard fist.

"Plenty!" he whispered. "Three whole divisions, and more on the way. And that reminds me, you remember your last report to Sir John? About the industrial maps you were making of Germany?"

The German hesitated for the briefest part of a second, and Combat, watching closely out the corner of his eye, was sure he saw a frown flicker across the man's brows.

"Of course, I remember," he said finally. "What about them?"

"I don't know," Combat said. "But in the excitement of finding you last night, I damn well forgot one of the reasons I came here. Just before I left Sir John gave me a sealed envelope to give to you if I found you alive. I was to destroy it once I was sure you were dead. I don't know what's in it. Sir John simply said that it had to do with your last report about the secret industrial maps you were preparing."

"Give it to me, quick!" the other said and half turned and held out his hand.

"Hell, I haven't got it on me, naturally," Combat said scornfully. "I hid it. I was taking no chances of getting caught today and searched. I've buried it. Is it permitted for us to leave here? To walk around a bit? I can dig it up."

"Of course, it's permitted!" the other said eagerly. "We do not have to be in the bunkhouse for another forty minutes. Besides, it is dangerous to talk too much in here. Let us go for a walk, eh?" WITHOUT WAITING for Combat to agree or disagree, the German got up and shuffled over to the bar and deposited his empty mug. Combat did the same, but as he let go of the mug a chilly thought rippled through his brain. He wondered if he'd ever taste beer again in this world—even the vile slop they served in the canteen. He wondered, and let it go at that, and shuffled out the door in the wake of the German. Once they were outside the man continued to play the role he thought he was playing to perfection.

"Let us not walk fast," he cautioned. "The swine guards might become suspicious. What direction?"

"This way," Combat grunted, and started off toward the left and the area of darkness over in back of the machine and tool building. The German grunted as though in surprise, but he fell into step with Combat. Just before they faded into the dark area Combat shot a swift glance back over his shoulder and a feeling of grim satisfaction oozed through him. For the present the German was playing a lone hand. No one was watching them, let alone attempting to follow them. Quickening his steps, Combat hurried deeper and deeper into the night-darkened area.

He wasn't exactly sure just what was in front of them, but he prayed from the bottom of his soul they wouldn't stumble into a prowling guard. The didn't and presently Combat spotted the thing he wanted. A small clump of bushes. He touched the

German's arm and circled around in back of it. Then he dropped to his knees.

"Give me a hand, Rollins," he whispered. "This stone is certainly damn heavy."

The German instantly obeyed and Combat heard the man suck air through his teeth. No sooner was the man on his knees than Combat snaked out the Luger he had been carrying under his shirt, next to his skin, and rammed the muzzle hard into the other's stomach.

"Relax, rat!" he grated. "This is a gun, and it wouldn't bother me a bit to blast your guts right out past your backbone. But it would bother you… plenty! A bullet in the guts hurts like hell, they tell me. Now we'll talk turkey. Keep your voice down."

"Good God, are you crazy, Combat?" came the gasping whisper. "Put down that gun! What the devil?"

Combat rammed the muzzle deeper in the flabby flesh.

"Well, well! Even know my name, eh?" he murmured.

"Don't be a fool!" the other breathed. "Of course I know your name! I…."

"Shut up, louse!" Combat hissed and rasped the knuckles of his other hand down the man's cheek. "You know it, sure. But Rollins *didn't*! He didn't ask me, and I didn't tell him. What happened to Rollins, square-head?"

"I… Rollins…?" the German stammered.

"Yeah, Rollins!" Combat grated. "The lad I met last night. That was his real name in a white man's country. I don't know what he was called in this pig-pen. Well, what happened to the fellow, damn you?"

"He was caught trying to enter the chemical plant," came the answer after a long pause. "He… he was shot. But I… I am only doing my duty. Do not kill me. I beg you, do not kill me!"

The sniveling, sobbing whisper of utter terror made Combat's stomach turn over in disgust. He wanted to smash the German's teeth down his throat, but he refrained from doing so. The man was also Combat's one and only ticket to freedom, perhaps.

"WHETHER YOU die is up to you," he told the man. "And paste this in your hat; I can spill out your guts all in stride, and think nothing of it. So if you want a break, want to live, then pay attention, and give me the right answers. How can I get out of here?"

"You can't," the German whimpered.

Combat jerked up the Luger and cracked him on the bridge of the nose, then rammed it right between his teeth to soft pedal any groan of pain.

"Wrong answer, Fritz!" he grated. "Try again, and make it good, or teacher will crack your teeth out!"

"But you can't, in those clothes!" the German moaned. "Only the guards are allowed outside the gates. You would have to get hold of a guard's uniform."

"How would *you* get one," Combat asked, "if you didn't want to die?"

"I don't know, I don't know!" the other whimpered. "Perhaps I would…."

"Would what?" Combat prompted with his lips *and* the Luger.

"Perhaps I would try to steal one through the window of the guards' hutment," the German said just a bit too quickly. "They keep their spare uniforms on hooks. If no one was looking you could reach through the window."

"And why wouldn't the guards inside be looking?" Combat asked softly.

"Why… why when the guard is changed every four hours," the man stammered. "You could do it. And then you wouldn't be challenged at the gate. The guards are allowed to go into the town when not on duty. Yes, I think you could do it easily."

Combat smiled in the darkness. He had been wondering, and now he knew. He knew damn well that the man impersonating poor old Rollins was a guard, himself. He tapped the Luger muzzle on the German's chest.

"*I* couldn't do it easily," he said. "But you could. And will. I'll be right close to you, and I'm a pip of a shot. Ever get a bullet in your spine? Now there is something that really hurts, buddy. Your whole body is filled with pain, yet your muscles are all paralyzed so that you can't do a thing about it. No, not even speak. Okay, when's the next change of guard?"

The guard shivered and seemed to have considerable difficulty in getting his tongue down off the roof of his mouth.

"At… at three o'clock," he finally gasped. "About fifteen minutes from now."

Combat knew the guardhouse was located directly in front of the workmen's quarters. Also that most of it was flooded with light. However, the rear third extended back out of the light into the darkness. But even there some light filtered from the windows. It was a long chance to take, but the German had spoken the truth about one thing. The only possible way to leave the Breslau Works was to leave as one of the guards. That way, or go out in a coffin—if that small courtesy was extended the dead, which it probably wasn't.

"Is your bunk near the rear end?" Combat suddenly shot at the man.

The gulping sound told him he had scored a bulls-eye.

"Y-y-yes, it is," the German said.

"Then it'll be your uniform, buddy," Combat said. "Okay, let's stroll over that way. And remember, a guy stays dead a hell of a long time."

Prodding the man with his Luger, Combat forced him up on his feet and started him off through the darkness toward the rear of the guards' sleeping quarters.

CHAPTER 14
DEATH CAN WAIT

THE PAIR took six steps, or maybe it was seven. Anyway, the German suddenly stumbled, and made as though to fall. But he didn't. A big man though he was, he spun like a flash of light and charged upward. Out of nowhere a gun appeared in his hand. It spat flame and sound, and Combat, hurling himself to the side, was blinded for a split second and a spear of white hot flame licked across his left side. Had he not leaped the instant the German stumbled he would now have a bullet in his guts.

But he had been prepared for the unexpected, and he had leaped.

"Take it, rat!" he grated, and squeezed lead.

The German took it, right smack between the eyes. He was stone dead and on his way to be furnace fuel for Satan before his stiff body hit the ground. Maybe it bounced. Combat didn't wait to see. The instant his bullet had struck home, he had whirled to the right and started running at top speed. In the comparative silence of the night the two shots had sounded like a couple of cannons going off. And before Combat had taken a dozen strides, lights began to spring up all over the place and the shouting of many voices echoed in the night air.

Changing his direction, Combat curved to the right, and around toward the workmen's hutments. He was still in the dark, unlighted area of the place, and unless searchlight beams began sweeping around he stood a fair chance of getting far enough away from the immediate vicinity to be spotted. However, his brain was a turmoil of conflicting thought as he plowed his way forward. Oddly enough, he was not too bitterly disappointed at the outcome of his little venture. Perhaps that was because deep down in his heart he had really believed that the chances of forcing the German to get him a guard's uniform had been really very slim indeed. Yet, it had been a chance, his only hope at the time, and he had been forced to take it.

"And who says this isn't a break?" he panted as he neared the guards' sleeping quarters. "The whole place is on its ear right now, and running around in circles, like me! But the guards are all out, and that makes it perfect. Bet I could ease in there and walk off with a cot, and nobody would see me."

It was fortunate for Combat, however, that none of the gods

reached down to take a piece of that bet, because he would have lost it, along with his shirt, and his life. Lost it, because when he was still some fifty yards from the guards' building, he saw that the place was flooded with light, and the inside lousy with hard-eyed men in uniform. He skidded to a halt, crouched down a bit and took a good look. It didn't make him happy at all, what he saw. Evidently the guards at Breslau had been thoroughly drilled for just such a situation. They were piling into their uniforms, strapping Lugers into place, and taking down powerful hand flashlights from the shelf above their cots. And not a few of them, who were all ready for action, were forming a fan-shaped formation out in front. In other words, the guards were going to sweep the area from one end to the other. They'd do a thorough job. "And every one of the rats knows just what to look for!" Combat whispered through clenched teeth. "A face that matches the one I'm wearing."

NO MATTER how he looked at it, he was in one hell of a fix. For the moment the darkness was his friend, but how long would that last? Any hope of reaching the guards building was definitely out, because it was plain to see that one line of guards was preparing to sweep south toward the main gate. And a second line was forming to sweep forward in the opposite direction toward the north. By and large, it was just like fishermen taking up the slack of their net and forcing the fish to swim toward the bank and shallow water where they could be virtually picked out by hand. Only in this case it was an advancing line of blood-letting Nazis—and one Bill Combat was the poor fish!

Fifteen minutes of freedom at the most! Not more than

fifteen minutes before that onsweeping line of guards would have him pinned against the high wire fence at the main gates. No they hadn't spotted him yet. Their flashlight beams sweeping back and forth over the ground were still a good sixty yards from him. He could keep falling back, falling back... until finally he had been herded up against the wire fence along with all the other poor workmen in the guards' path. There he would be picked out, and then... curtains!

He cursed softly, gripped his Luger tighter, and moved to his left and away from the cluster of buildings. If by any miracle he could skirt the far right end of the advancing line he could then slip back into the area already covered. And then the vacated guards' building would be his to investigate at his leisure.

Hope burned fiercely within him, but as he snaked farther and farther to the left that flame grew dimmer and dimmer. Some three hundred yards away was a fair-sized open space with not a single shrub or tree to mar it. Once he was in that open area a swinging flashlight beam could pick him out for a perfect Luger target. And even as he peered that way, a few lights sprang into being along one side of the flat open area, and his hopes dropped to a new low. The area was the flying field, and with those damn lights on he'd be no more conspicuous crossing it than he would be taking part in the Stork Club floor show back in little old New York. In other words, the location of that damn flying field cut off his escape in that direction.

At that moment, however, it was as though the gods looked down at him, and said, "What the hell! Let's give the sucker just one more break, eh?"

He managed to haul the plane
clear and go zooming up
towards the overcast sky.

Anyway, above the noise of shouting men Combat heard the throbbing drone of an airplane engine. Even as he raised his head the drone died away and the high-keyed whine of wings and struts in the wind took its place. In nothing flat he spotted the wing and tail lights of the ship. Three spots of color backgrounded by the black sky came swinging down toward the landing field. A single bank of flood lights flashed into being, and Combat dropped flat as their reflected glow went racing across the surrounding countryside. But though the slashing rays of light came close to giving him a permanent case of heart failure, they rekindled the tiny flame of hope within him. As he dropped he saw the deep irrigation ditch some twenty yards to his left rear. The ditch took a slightly zigzag course to a point close to the single hangar on the field.

Realization and action became one for Combat. He started rolling over and over in the grass, praying hard that the guards sixty yards away would be too intent upon watching the landing plane and would not see the movement his rolling body made in the scraggly grass. If he could reach that hangar unobserved, his chances of skirting the far side of the field and the right end of the guard line were practically doubled. His rolling body seemed suddenly to drop off the lip of the world, and in the next split second he was flat on his back in six inches of cold muddy water. Twisting over and scrambling up on all fours, he went scampering, spider style, along the irrigation ditch, keeping to its sloping side and out of the water as much as possible.

IT TOOK him three minutes to reach the end, where the ditch shallowed out into marsh land, but it could have been three years from the way his heart hammered against his ribs and the blood pounded in his temples. Not daring to stand up for a look around, he deliberately dropped flat and then slowly wormed his way up over the lip of the ditch and onto hard ground some twenty-five yards in back of the hangar. Still playing snake-belly, he wiggled forward until he was up against the far corner of the hangar. There he paused for a few seconds to jam his heart down out of his throat and drag blessed air into his lungs. Then, as sounds came to him, he stuck his head around the corner and took a look.

Out in the center of the field stood a Nazi Air Force two-seater Arado A R 95. A group of guards and some high rankers at Breslau stood around it, and as far as Combat could make out, everybody seemed to be talking at the same time.

"Sounds as if they're excited about something," he murmured.

Two figures were angrily pushing their way out of the group. One he recognized as Colonel Stoltz, the commandant at Breslau. The other figure, stalking along half a pace or so in front of Stoltz, snapped Combat's parted lips to a thin grim line and unconsciously made him bring up his Luger to draw a bead on the figure... who was well out of the Luger's range. The stalking man was Hermann Peiplow, chief of Nazi Intelligence, and the sight of him was final confirmation for Combat, if final confirmation were needed. The guess he'd made the instant he had spotted the perfectly good middle fingernail on the German's left hand had been absolutely correct. The Germans had known of every step he made. Yeah, beginning all the way back in London, in Sir John's office, no doubt. And now Peiplow had arrived to sit in at the killing.

"Only it isn't working out that way... yet!" Combat grated and beat down the urge to rush out there and plant a Luger bullet where it would do the Allies one hell of a lot of good.

With no little regret he crouched where he was and watched Peiplow and Stoltz stride toward the main building of the Works, and the mess of guards who trailed along behind them. Once they were out of sight Lady Luck would throw her arms wide and embrace him with his great break. His avenue of escape would be wide open. He could skirt the far side of the field and then double back into the area the guard line had covered. Then into the vacant guard house, grab the first uniform he saw, and then....

And then common reasoning kicked his risky plans higher than a kite. The pilot of the plane out on the field had revved his engine and was slowly taxiing the ship toward the hangar. A guard on each wingtip helped the pilot, and Combat wanted to dance a jig of joy, laugh out loud. Fate could give you some awful belts below the belt, but Fate could also be a hell of a swell guy on occasion.

"You guys know what you can do with your guard uniforms!" Combat chuckled softly. "I won't be needing one. Me, I'm nuts about this flying business!"

As the last slid off his lips, he straightened up a bit and set himself. The plane had reached the short strip of tarmac and was being swung around so that its nose was pointed out across the field. Combat waited until the pilot had cut his engine and climbed to the ground, then, like a flash of water-and-mud-soaked lightning, he darted out from around the corner of the hangar and confronted the three Germans.

"My pals!" he said with a short laugh. "Down on your bellies and hands over your head. Fast!"

THE THREE Germans blinked and looked very astounded and unhappy. Then one of the guards dropped flat as directed. The other guard gurgled in his throat and tugged for his Luger. Combat leaped forward and drilled him through the head. The pilot yelled and lunged for Combat bare-handed. The Yank simply whipped his gun sideways a couple of inches and got the man in the stomach. Before the pilot hit the tarmac Combat was in the cockpit of the two-seater, flipping up the ignition switch and banging the booster magneto crank.

Call it murder, cold blooded murder. Call it anything you wish. But Bill Combat called it his only hope to get away from Breslau. So that is the reason he twisted in the seat and planted a bullet in the skull of the one live guard as the man started to push himself up on his hands and knees.

A split second later the roar of the plane's engine had drowned out the echo of Combat's final shot. It also drowned out the wild bellow of many voices, and the crack and snarl of Lugers and Mauser rifles as Combat sent the reconnaissance plane rocketing across the small field.

With still half the width of the field in front of him, he managed to haul the plane clear and go zooming up toward the overcast sky. As he zoomed he twisted his head and glanced down back at the ground. A swarm of uniformed guards was rushing out onto the field, shooting wildly at him as they ran. And somebody had manned a searchlight.

Combat laughed harshly, thumbed his nose, and leveled off at the top of his zoom and started zigzagging in a general northerly direction. But that's all he did… just started northward.

A picture of Rollins rose up before his eyes. Utter fatigue was on the British Intelligence man's face, then hope—wild hope— then the cold despair that must have been there when he was caught; and then the glassy look of death when that German bullet sent him to another world.

The picture of all that was too much for Combat. It burned

his blood, seared his brain, and banished all thoughts of France, England, and himself. He swore aloud, slammed the plane around in a dime turn, and went roaring down toward the guard-spotted field in a prop-howling power dive.

"The five already dead are not enough for you, Rollins, old man!" he shouted. "So I'll get you some more!"

He punctuated the last by jabbing the trigger trips forward. The four fixed guns, two in the nose and one in each of the lower wings, spattered slashing death earthward, and guards started taking dives all over the place. Those that were not picked off wheeled around and set sprinting records for distances in all directions. Finally there was nothing on the field that could move. Combat kicked rudder and dished his last burst of bullets right straight at the searchlight as its operator tried frantically to keep him in its spot.

The light went out. Combat relaxed pressure on the trigger trips and zoomed once more for the clouds. How many were dead below he had no way of telling.

"Plenty of the rats, though, Rollins," he muttered. "But still not enough to make it all square. But I'll stay in and pitch as long as I can, old man!"

CHAPTER 15
BLACK WINGS AT DAWN

THE LAST tremor of the escape's excitement draining from his body, Combat nosed the two-seater up into the layer of clouds and went through to come out under a canopy of faintly blinking stars. Over China way, the sun of a new dawn was hot on the coattails of fleeing night. Already the first dim ribbons of grey light were creeping across the slowly fading stars.

Leveling off, Combat set a course almost due west and relaxed slowly in the seat. He was a free man. He had a bullet crease along his left side, but it was no more than a scratch and hardly ached at all. He had a good plane under him, and a good fourteen thousand feet of air under the plane. So what?

"So you'd better do something about it, quick!" he grunted aloud. "Just about now the Breslau wireless and radio station is working hot and heavy, and in a little while these here skies are going to be full of Nazi pilots looking for you."

His eyes caught a dull milky blur below him and considerably off to his left. Too often had he seen that sort of thing not to be able to tab it in a flash. In a few words, the engine in the nose was making a hell of a roar, and airplane "ears" on the ground had picked up the sound. And powerful search light beams were beating themselves against the under side of the cloud layer in a futile effort to pick him up.

Shoving on left rudder pedal, he swung around toward the south, then lifted the nose and started climbing. When he had reached top ceiling for that type of ship he leveled off and continued flying southward for some twenty minutes or more. Then he slowly eased off the engine, slanted the ship nose down a shade and went gliding around and back toward the northeast.

For a good twenty-five minutes he managed to keep his glide above the clouds, but by that time he was many, many miles from the spot where the airplane "ears" had first picked him up. Also, if his more or less blind flying and blind gliding calculations were correct, he was many, many miles closer to his next objective—the German-Dutch frontier town of Kleve.

Kleve was the next mile-post in his crazy, cockeyed journey that had started at Sir John's War Office building office. Wherever good old Rollins was, now, he need not feel that his months of mental and physical torture at Breslau had been in vain. It was the dead Rollins who was sending him toward Kleve. It was Rollins who had told him of the assembly plant at Kleve, and of the crates of mysterious parts that had been shipped there from the Breslau Works. Yes, it had been Rollins, too, who made it possible for Combat to link up his strange North Sea adventure with the work at Breslau. And it had been Rollins who had given Combat the real truth about the mysterious secret of the Siegfried Line.

"So you didn't die in vain, old man," he whispered softly and raised his eyes to the fast fading stars. "I… I guess I brought death to you, Rollins, but if I come out of this on top your name is going to get all the credit."

LOWERING HIS gaze, he shrugged aside the depressing thoughts and concentrated grimly on his flying. The light in the east was coming up fast, though it was unquestionably pretty dark down there below the cloud layer. The point was, though, that if once again his calculations were right on the beam, he should be mighty close to the Kleve sector. What he planned to do, if and when he made an unobserved landing close by, he did not know at the moment. Maybe he'd find everything he hoped to find, and maybe he'd find nothing. There really wasn't anything to plan, for the simple reason that he had not the foggiest idea of what confronted him. He was simply a guy high up in the air over enemy country.

And for the present he could pick his spot. He would pick Kleve, because of all that had come to pass.

"So now we'll take a look-see," he grunted and went nosing down through the clouds. "Must find out where the hell I am, anyway."

It was considerably lighter under the clouds than he expected it to be. In fact, there was sufficient dawn light for him to obtain a fairly good view of the shadow-tinted landmarks below. In ten seconds he spotted a familiar twist in the Rhine and the Wesel, and in another five seconds he spotted the Kleve sector and the Dutch frontier, dead ahead of him and below.

"Take a bow, pal," he chuckled. "You've hit it right on the nose. You're getting better."

It was a modest compliment and well deserved, but high up in that far off place the gods of war had a swell laugh for themselves.

A dozen powerful searchlights flashed into being and sent their dazzling rays straight up to wipe the pleased grin off Bill Combat's face. He cursed and jumped hard on right rudder to whirl his ship over and around in a dime turn. But all it got him was another half-dozen beams cutting their white swath up through the dark sky. And a couple of seconds later Combat was the most startled man in the world. From out of nowhere, on three sides, came a flock of small dark shadows ripping in at him and spitting jetting tongues of flame.

Only they weren't mere shadows. They were German pursuit planes. And the spitting jets of flame were accompanied by lots of bullets that whined and crackled around his ears. Nor did one of the on-rushing pilots have to lean out of his pit, and shout, "We've been waiting for you to show up around this neck of the woods, Mister!" Combat knew it without being told and he felt very lousy in the pit of his stomach.

"Some day I *will* give the Nazis some credit for brains, I hope!" he breathed fiercely. "Then maybe I won't get in trouble so often!"

That was the last word that flipped off his lips for the next five minutes. That is, save for a series of curses that would make a sea pirate sit up and smile. Frankly, he didn't have time to put words together that would make sense. It seemed that practically the entire Nazi Air Force was buzzing and slamming around him. Yeah, give the Nazis credit for some brains. Herman Peiplow, no doubt. The German chief of Intelligence had undoubtedly added two and two and gotten four. Which meant that he'd figured Rollins had learned something about Kleve and had passed the tip on to Combat.

So plenty of planes had gone aloft to patrol the skies and wait for him. Hell, maybe his trick bit of flying to get there hadn't been any trick at all. Perhaps airplane "ears" had followed every rev of his prop, and no effort had been made to go up after him by plane or searchlight once it was realized he was heading in the direction of Kleve. Right! If he came down at Kleve there would be the reception committee of bullet-spitting wings. And if by chance he started out over the Dutch border on his way back to England the "reception committee" would still be there to spoil his homecoming.

A RECEPTION committee... and death. Light, crazy thoughts flickered through Combat's brain as he hurled and belted his ship all over the sky, and let fly at anything that rushed across in front of his nose. But even so his heart was a cold lump in his chest. And he knew full well it would not be long before something would let go... and it would be *him*. Sure, he was a crack pilot. Give him the top rating. Say he was the greatest pilot in the world. It still added up to nothing better than a glass of stale beer. Six, or even a dozen best pilots in the world couldn't have stood a chance against that skyful of Nazi planes. So what chance did Combat have?

He had none. True, he sent four planes blazing down into eternity but he was doomed to be sunk, and he was sunk. A burst of bullets smashed into his engine and practically tore off the cowling. The power plant sputtered and coughed and vibrated so violently it seemed ready to leap from its bearers in the next split second.

Flashing out his free hand, Combat snapped off the ignition and hauled the throttle all the way back. With his other hand still on the controls, he sticked and booted the plane over and down into a tight spin. And a hell of a lot of good *that* did him! He dropped a thousand feet in nothing flat. In fact, he got well down below the milling German planes. But those German pilots were not flying steam rollers. Two of them came down like a couple of bats out of hell. Their guns yammered and snarled, and Combat's spinning plane took on a terrific load of hot lead.

And then, suddenly, before his horrified eyes, it happened!

A tiny puff of smoke belched out from the right side of the nose. Almost instantly a small tongue of flame appeared. The wind caught it and spread it out to sheet size and sent it whipping back toward the cockpit. In a dazed, abstract sort of way Combat knew that an explosive bullet had nailed a gas feed line, split it and set fire to the raw gas in the tube. He was on fire. On fire and hurtling earthward at terrific speed.

Somehow his brain managed to whip his paralyzed muscles into action. Shielding his face from the leaping flame, he kicked the ship into a side-slip on the opposite wing. That drove the flame upward and away from him. All he had to do, now, was to hold the ship in the side-slip and pray to God the flames wouldn't melt the engine bolts loose so that the power plant would drop clear and throw the rest of the ship haywire. That's all he had to do, because once he was close enough to the ground he could whip the ship over, make a fast stall landing, and take a chance on getting out of the wreck before the flames got him.

Yes, that was all, but the gods had decided to give him the works, so he didn't succeed in doing anything. The ground, a tree top to be exact, came up at him too fast. He saw it too late to jam his plane past it. And then he didn't see anything but lots and lots of beautiful colored lights that mysteriously changed into many hands that grabbed hold of him and flung him out into nothing at all.

CHAPTER 16
WINGS FOR A CORPSE

" SO HELP me, I'll never take another drink as long as I live!—God, what a head I've got!"

The moaned words floated back into Bill Combat's ears and stirred something in his brain. He realized that it was his own voice that had spoken, but he didn't give a damn. He'd spoken the truth. The squadron gang could go on all the benders they wanted, but not him. Nix! Never again. To hell with it! The four heads he had—and all four pounding to beat hell—weren't worth it. He....

His thoughts suddenly merged into blank confusion. He had pried open his eyes to find himself staring up at a faint, early dawn-tinted sky. He tried to think and it hurt like hell. Had he passed out on the flying field? Surely his orderly would have gone looking for him when he didn't show up at his hutment. He... A sound! What the hell? A sound like running water. It *was* running water. Where in hell was he anyway?

He tried to sit up and almost made it, but his insides seemed to let go and his body dropped back. Something was wrong, wrong as hell. His fast clearing brain whipped him into increased effort. He made a sitting position this time, though a couple of thousand white hot needles stabbed him in all parts of his body. Blank-eyed, he stared at totally unfamiliar scenery, but maybe that was because it was still dark. Dawn was still low down in the east. He was sitting squarely in the middle of a beaten-down clump of bushes. He was close to the bank of a fairly good-sized river, and the water was tearing along in a hell of a hurry. The river bank near him looked as if a gang had gone over it with pick and shovel. It was all torn up. A patch of small trees had been sliced off clean, a foot from the ground, and the trunks lay every which way. And a bush clump had been neatly uprooted, turned upside down, and left that way, its dirt-clogged roots pointed at the sky. And there was something white and rumpled on the bank, then he saw a second piece of rumpled cloth, and a third. And, holy smokes, a wheel fastened to a fire-charred hunk of wood was sticking up out of the water close to the bank! A wheel that must have—"

"A plane wheel!"

The echo of his own voice seemed to pull a curtain aside in Combat's brain, then everything came rushing back to him like flood waters pouring over a broken dam. Oblivious to the pain each motion caused, he scrambled up onto his feet and stood swaying unsteadily on his pins. Yeah, he remembered all, now. It was no "morning-after" a bender.

"And I'm alive!" he muttered thickly. "Boy, did somebody get a hell of a cheating!"

Impulsively he bent back his head, looked upward and searched the heavens with his eyes. The ones who had been cheated were no longer up there. Figuring they had made a damn good job of things, they had returned to their respective dromes to call it a day. Or rather, call it a night. A lad just doesn't go on living when he crashes in flames.

Parts of his crashed plane were floating on the surface of the water, close into shore and out of the main current. By peering hard he could just barely make out the engine, half buried in the muddy bottom not fifteen feet from where he stood. What should have happened, but didn't, made his knees weak, and his stomach to feel as if it was loaded with buckshot. He sank down at the river's edge and stayed there a full five minutes.

AT THE end of five minutes, however, pain or no pain, he was automatically roused into action. From off to his right and low down over the river came the roar of a Mercedes engine. He didn't even stop to see if he could spot the plane. He didn't even want to. He knew it was there, and why. Hitler's boys always like to make sure they really have spilled blood, whether it be civilian or soldier blood. So some lad was hedge-hopping down the river's surface for a look at the spot where he had crashed.

And as Combat dived away from the river bank and burrowed like a hunted fox into the heart of a thorny thicket, he realized for the first time what his first glance at the sky should have conveyed to him. He hadn't been out such a very long time.

Huddled motionless in his nest of thorns, Combat listened to the roar of the Mercedes coming closer and closer. Then suddenly the roar lessened a bit, and he knew what that meant. The plane's pilot had spotted his wreckage and was slowing up to circle the area and take a good look. And that's exactly what the pilot did. He took more than a good look. He circled around so low that Combat, looking at him through the dense maze of thorn branches, could have reached up one hand and punched a landing gear tire as the ship skipped by.

For ten solid minutes he was forced to crouch there in the thicket, stabbed by thorns in a hundred places, and not a little bit light in the head from pain, while the German pilot circled around long enough to satisfy himself that Combat must have died in the crash.

Not until the sound of the engine was a faint moan in the distance did Combat stir from his hiding place. And even then he did so more or less reluctantly. His strength badly sapped, his brain foggy from weariness and fatigue. His whole body filled with pain from head to toe, he was almost content to stay right there in his bed of thorns.

But that part of a fighter which still functions when everything about him has gone to pot forced Combat out of that thorn thicket and up onto his feet. The sky was getting brighter and brighter, and he didn't have the faintest idea where he was. The river there was either the Rhine or the Wesel, probably the latter because it wasn't very wide. And it flowed from left to right, so he was facing south. The light of dawn on his left proved that, of course. But it meant that Kleve was somewhere to his right. Maybe a few miles, maybe fifty.

"Up and at 'em, slob!" he growled. "What the hell, you didn't break a damn bone, did you? Are you waiting for Lady Luck to lead you by the hand?"

With a shrug, he moved some fifty yards away from the river's bank, and keeping it on his left, started wearily across country, more or less groping his way through the semi-darkness and stumbling to his knees every dozen steps or so as he tripped over a root or a rock. He did not feel very hungry but he craved a cigarette. There was a pack of German cigarettes in his pocket but he didn't dare light one, for two reasons. First, because the silence all about him seemed to act as a warning of some kind. Somehow it seemed to convey to him the hunch that he was not in territory so deserted as it appeared, and the flare of a match might bring trouble. The second reason, however, was the most important. His crash ripped clothes smelled to high heaven of raw gas and oil. If he lighted a cigarette, he might possibly light himself.

A SOUND to his right and ahead suddenly brought him to a halt. He cocked an ear in that direction and scowled. If he were in the Maine woods he would be able to identify it at once. He'd say that it was a saw mill starting up, and be right. But here in Germany, in a section of it where there wasn't a tree over thirty feet high at the most, he knew such a guess wasn't worth a damn.

"Then it must be some kind of machinery," he grunted. "Gears meshing, or something."

He listened a couple of minutes more, and then, when the buzzing sound ceased, he started moving more to his right, toward a fairly good-sized patch of woods. The moment he entered the woods the faint light of dawn was cut off by the maze of branches over his head.

No less than a couple of hundred tree trunks got in his way, and then, without warning, he banged his shins against a huge rock. He cursed softly and started to feel his way around it... and stopped short. It wasn't any rock he had stumbled into. It was something made of metal. Carefully he felt it over with his hands and strained his eyes for a look at it in the bad light. Suddenly he knew, and realization sent a clammy chill rippling down his spine.

He had bumped up against a small, high speed armored tank there in the woods. Parked next to it was a second tank. He moved past it to stumble against a third, and a fourth. By then, sufficient dawn light filtered down through the maze of leafless branches and he was able to observe the real purpose of the woods—a purpose certainly never intended by Nature.

His guess was a shot in the dark, of course, but there were at least four hundred tanks parked in that area. Parked and ready to go, yet not a single soldier attending them.

"And what would five hundred tanks be doing, hiding up here in these woods?" Combat breathed and his heart pumped with excitement. "What would they be doing there? That's easy. Pal, your hunch back there at Breslau is beginning to show a profit. The bums! Secret of the Siegfried Line, huh? Nuts!"

He spoke the last in scornful tone, but just the same his heart contracted a bit, and goose pimples came out on his skin. The light of understanding was burning brighter in his brain. What had seemed like a wild guess back there at Breslau was becoming more and more the cold truth. The true picture was unfolding before his eyes.

"But there's just one part missing," he muttered, and stared at the row after row of shadow-shrouded tanks. "The secret of Breslau that'll make a *Blitzkreig* through Holland *really* work. Because that's what these tanks mean. A smash through Holland while the Allies are waiting for the expected smash at the Maginot Line. Yeah, there's one part of the picture missing. No matter how many troops and tanks and stuff Hitler has hidden up here on the Frontier, the Dutch are sure to be able to hold him off until we can come tearing up through Belgium to lend a hand. He…."

Combat paused, scowled hard and racked his brain for the answer.

"Could it be a bluff stab at Holland?" he breathed. "To pull our troops up from the Maginot Line and Belgian Frontier? Nope, that's out. The Maginot fortifications would hold for a hell of a while with even a skeleton force manning them. No, Hitler can't be that crazy!"

FURTHER SPECULATION was cut off by the return of the buzzing sound. It came from a very short distance away, to his right. He promptly ceased having any interest in the tanks and set off at as rapid a gait as the underbrush and stones would allow. It took him some ten minutes to reach the far side of the woods. And when he reached it he found himself staring out at the most cockeyed, most grotesque, most amazing scene his eyes had ever gazed upon.

The first thing he saw was a row of long, low-roofed sheds built back under the trees. The parts not actually under the trees were strewn with cut branches and shrubs for camouflage effect. At the near end of the area were three sets of narrow gauge tracks that lead due east over the countryside. On each track were some twenty to twenty-five small flat-cars. And mounted on each flatcar, and completely shrouded with camouflage material, was a Henschel two-seater of the parasol wing type. One by one the little cars were being pulled over the track by a small gasoline engine that gave off a buzzing sound.

Like a man in a trance, Combat watched one of the little

engines coasting down the track from the east. It slowed up and bumped gently against one of the plane-laden flatcars. German air mechanics leaped forward to couple the engine to the car, then, as an officer barked an order, they fell upon the flatcar and gave it a push to start it rolling. Then the dinkey little engine buzzed it away out of sight over a slight rise of ground.

Several times, as Combat watched the cockeyed proceedings, he brushed a hand across his eyes by way of making sure he was seeing straight. He even pinched himself, and the sharp pain told him there wasn't any kidding about it. There before him was the mysterious Kleve "assembly" plant. Base 12, no doubt, that received the Breslau parts that Rollins had seen ready for rail shipment.

"It doesn't make sense!" Combat muttered. "Why rail those ships toward the frontier? Why not fly them up if there's a field farther along? Maybe I'm nuts, but…."

He shrugged away the last and peered hard at the Henschel nearest him. Because of the mass of camouflage spread over it he could see little more than enough of its outline to recognize it definitely as a Henschel—exactly like the type he'd seen zinging across the tips of a tramp steamer's masts in the North Sea.

Suddenly, though, his eyes focussed on parts of the plane that were entirely strange to him.

Small tanks completely covered by copper coils were fastened to the belly of the ship between the landing wheels. The coils led back to the tail, where two of them flanged out like the mouths of small vacuum cleaners, and tilted downward slightly.

"Looks like a ship fitted up for cotton dusting against the

bollweevil," he grunted. "Only they don't grow cotton up this way. And those are *military* ships!"

In his eagerness to get a better look at the planes mounted on the small flat-cars, he moved forward a dozen steps or so. A figure suddenly rose right up out of the ground, twenty feet to his right.

"Halt!"

The order cracked against his eardrums. He jerked his head that way, and looked straight down the muzzle of a Mauser rifle held steady in the big paws of a bull-necked Nazi soldier!

CHAPTER 17
A GROUNDED EAGLE

COMBAT'S FIRST impulse was to drop flat and go for the Luger he still carried in his pocket. Perhaps he might have given in to that impulse if he had had the chance. But he didn't get the chance. A second German soldier materialized right in back of him, and the muzzle of another Mauser was rammed between his shoulder blades. He sighed and slowly raised both hands above his head. What the hell, he had at least come close, if that was any consolation.

As one soldier kept a Mauser against his back, the other advanced cautiously, frisked him, and relieved him of his Luger.

"Who are you? What are you doing here?"

A crazy, inane crack started up Combat's throat. But on second thought he choked it back. Maybe he still had a card left to play. At any rate it was as good a stall for time as any he

119

could think of at the moment. He looked blank, and allowed his mouth to sag a bit.

"I don't know," he mumbled. "Who am I? Where am I?"

That completely baffled the soldier because he most certainly didn't know the first part of Combat's question. He stared questioningly over Combat's shoulder at his pal. His pal spoke.

"We will take him to *Herr Kammandant,* at once," he said. "He will know best how to question him. March, you, in front of me!"

There wasn't anything else Combat could do, considering the situation. As the soldiers marched him over toward one of the low-roofed buildings, Combat tried to get an even better look at his surroundings, but they didn't give him much of a chance. However, dawn was well up by now and his practiced eyes sweeping about the nearby countryside spotted many signs that totalled up to a dull ache in his heart. If the Nazis were masters of anything, it was the fine art of camouflaging. Everything his eyes rested upon added to that conviction. Cleverly concealed in the area was a powerful mechanized army, complemented by scores of Henschels seemingly fitted with cotton dusting equipment.

And then he was shoved through a door and into the office of the slate-eyed, flabby-faced commander of the joint.

"We found him trying to sneak out of the woods, *Herr Kommandant,*" one of die soldiers announced. "So we have brought him to you at once. He states he does not know who he is, or where he is. We have taken this Luger from him."

The guard placed the gun on the desk and then stepped back to await further orders. The Commander ignored him.

He bored Combat with his blazing eyes.

"Well, tell me, swine!" he suddenly boomed. "What is your name? Where do you come from? And why are you here? You wear a workman's clothes, eh? Perhaps you have escaped from some labor battalion. Well, speak up!"

Combat plucked at his lower lip and slowly moved his head from side to side.

"I do not know," he mumbled in low German. "I do not know anything. I cannot remember."

The Commander puffed out his cheeks and looked angry enough to reach across the desk and smash a fist into Combat's face. Then, suddenly, there came a sharp exclamation to Combat's right. A German flying officer he had not noticed upon entering the office suddenly leaped out of a chair and came forward quickly. He bent close to Combat and sniffed. His eyes grew wide in dumbfounded disbelief.

"There is the smell of gasoline and oil about him," the German exploded at the Commandant. "And his clothes are torn and covered with mud. *Ach du lieber Gott!* It cannot be! It is impossible!"

"What is impossible, *Herr Kapitan?*" the Commandant demanded as Combat's heart sank.

The German flying captain was so excited he couldn't talk for a moment. He gazed wide-eyed at the Yank as though he were a ghost. Then the words came in a terrific rush.

"This man is lying, *Herr Kommandant!*" he cried. "He is the pilot of the plane we shot down not two hours ago. It is impossible, yet it is so. He lives. He is alive!"

"Mein Gott!" the Commandant rumbled in his throat. "Can it be so, *ja?* But you are the very man who flew over the spot, *Mein Kapitan.* You said yourself there was nothing but shreds of the wreck floating down the river!"

"I know what I said," murmured the pilot still staring at Combat, "but I made a mistake. *Ja,* did I not make a mistake, *Herr* Combat?"

His name was shot at him so unexpectedly the Yank was wholly unprepared. Too late his body started slightly, and his eyes flickered. He tried to cover it up instantly.

"Who is *Herr* Combat, *Herr Kapitan?*" he asked thickly.

The ruse didn't work. The German flying officer laughed gleefully and excitedly.

"He must be this Combat we were ordered to find and destroy," he said to the senior officer. "If I may suggest it, I believe it would be wise to keep him closely guarded until we make sure. That can be done very easily."

The Base *Kommandant* tried to stare right into Combat's brain. He nodded shortly.

"But, of course," he grunted. "I will phone at once. Take the prisoner away and lock him up. Tell the Sergeant of the Guard he is to be watched constantly. If he even *thinks* about escaping, shoot him in the stomach. Take him away!"

WITH THE heel of Fate crunching down on his last hope Combat permitted the two soldiers to march him outside and down the row of low-roofed sheds to a small, squat and very solidly built building. A barred door was pushed open and Combat shoved inside. He stumbled a few steps in the bad light, banged up against a bench and fell across it. Wearily he picked himself up and sat down. The two soldiers leered at him between the door bars. Then one left while the other remained, not taking his eyes off Combat for a second, and holding his rifle at the alert.

During the next half hour it seemed that practically the entire personnel of the place paraded by to have a look at him. Finally, though, the novelty was gone, and there was only the alert guard outside the door. Pushing the bench to the wall so he could rest his back against it, Combat shut his eyes to keep out the truth and once more carefully placed the pieces of the crazy puzzle in their correct spots. There was one piece still missing. Rather, one piece that didn't exactly fit.

Assuming that Hitler was going to try a *Blitzkreig* against Holland and cut straight through to the sea, thus flanking the Allied armies in France... just how in hell did he expect to accomplish it before the Allies could stop him? Men, guns, tanks, and so forth wouldn't be enough. The Dutch fortifications, aided by the flooded lowlands, would stop the advance, or at least slow it down for three or four days. And in that time the Allied armies, and Belgian forces, would be up there to say, "Oh, no you don't, Adolf," and be able to make it stick.

So there was one piece of the puzzle missing, and he was positive those camouflage-covered Henschel planes represented that piece. But that was the only part of which he was sure. The point was, how were those planes going to do any more than what planes ordinarily did during a drive? That was to observe, strafe enemy positions, drop bombs, and raise merry hell in general.

But it was *obvious* that those Henschel were going to play some very, very special part. They were the *Blitzkreig*, the real secret of the puzzle—the difference between failure and success. Sure! All that granted. But *what* part were they to play? Combat didn't know, and his weary brain ran out of guesses in a short time.

When that moment arrived, when he let go of himself for the slight fraction of a second, the little demons of misery, remorse, and defeat came rushing in upon him from all sides with their needle-sharp spears. His spirits went all the way down, and once again he sort of half-wished that the crash had done a real job of it. He wasn't of any damn use to anybody, now.

Not even to the Germans, except, perhaps, as Exhibit A. Step right up, *mein Herren,* and have a look!

"WELL, WELL, my dear Captain Combat! I believe the last time was at Hamburg, was it not?"

The smooth, purring voice dragged Combat up from the depths of bitter reverie, and pried his eyes open. A big man stood just inside the cell door. He had a flat cruel face, and small black eyes that glittered brightly. He was Hermann Peiplow, chief of German Intelligence. When Combat didn't speak, the man laughed and waggled a thick finger at him.

"You are surprised, eh?" he murmured. "Or are you playing the dumb role you tried on *Herr Kommandant?* If so, you can stop now. They phoned me and I came up here in the fastest plane I could order. To tell you the truth, I hardly dared believe it could be so. But perhaps I forgot how often Fate has been kind to you in the past, eh? *Ach,* it is like a dream come true!"

The German let out a long sigh of complete contentment and grinned at Combat. The Yank met his gaze, and grinned himself. "Unless you are going to shoot me on the spot, *Herr* Peiplow," he said, "could I have a drink first?"

The other raised a hand and snapped his finger.

"Guard!" he roared without turning his head. "A bottle of *schnapps* for *Herr* Combat, at once!"

Combat was a bit surprised to see the guard duck away out of sight without so much as closing the door. The surprise lasted but the flickering of a second. Hermann Peiplow held a Luger in his other hand. He couldn't possibly have missed the heart of a gnat at the distance, let alone the heart of a man. Combat swallowed his rising hope and looked into the German's eyes.

"Thanks," he said. "But you wouldn't shoot the glass out of a pal's hand, would you? It's been done to me before."

"You may have all the *schnapps* you wish, *Herr* Combat," Peiplow said with a smile. "The country for which you fight would never admit it, but we Germans do admire courage, and brains. True, you lack in the latter considerably. But you do have courage, *Herr* Combat, and a certain amount of resourcefulness. I salute you, and quite frankly admit I—I enjoyed your escape from Breslau. It was quite thrilling. So, naturally, I am only too glad to grant your requests."

"What, no firing squad?" Combat murmured.

"Most assuredly so, when it comes time," Hermann Peiplow

quickly corrected. "Meantime, though, enjoy your *schnapps*. Ah, and here it is."

Peiplow took the bottle from the guard who entered the cell at that moment and handed it to Combat with a flourish.

"*Ach*, yes," he grunted. "Meantime, enjoy the *schnapps*. We will meet again very shortly."

Turning, the chief of German Intelligence more or less booted the gaping guard out the door ahead of him and slammed it shut. Without glancing back in he stalked away. Combat held up the bottle, idly read the label, and sighed heavily.

"And the doomed man had a bottle of *schnapps!*" he grunted. "Nuts! Why didn't I have him make it Scotch!"

CHAPTER 18
HIGHWAY OF THE DAMNED

THE SUN had gone down out of sight over the western lip of the world. Combat had watched it through the door of his cell, and when the last flaming ray had faded to a muddy orange, then to nothing, he shivered and clenched his two fists in a helpless gesture. His nerves were like a fine wire that couldn't even stand another half ounce of strain. For hours he had held himself in check because he believed Hermann Peiplow's failure to return a part of the man's little game—to wear him down to a frazzle. Food had been sent to him, and all the *schnapps* he wanted. But he hadn't wanted much, because if there was one thing he must do it was to keep a clear head.

However, the nerves of even the toughest of men have their

limits, and Combat was close to his limit. All during the long, dragged-out hours he had heard a hundred and one different sounds, all of which were caused by furious activity. Through the door he could see nothing but a stretch of rolling ground, and it darn near drove him nuts to be forced to sit on the cell bench and not be able to step close to the door for a look at what was going on. And that he was not able to do. Maybe a hundred times he tried to get near the door, but each time the guard's Mauser snaked through between the bars and spoke the universal language of a gun. It said, "Back up, Mister, and stay put, or I'll spit lead in your guts!"

True, a couple of Nazi planes had ripped by across his narrow range of vision, but nothing else. He heard the engines of lots of planes, and many times the odd buzzing sound the flatcar engines made. There was the rattle of tanks, too, and of armored cars. And much, much tramping of hobnail boots on the ground. Each new sound was just another tooth of the blunt saw clipping across his nerves. And now that the sun had gone down, and night was creeping across Europe, he felt more completely lost and defeated than ever.

One half of his brain egged him on to rush the barred door, and invite the guard's bullet. At least it would be *something*. Why not die now and have the damn thing over with? He had lost, hadn't he? Why give Peiplow the satisfaction of prolonging his agony? Hadn't the louse assured him that the final pay-off would be the firing squad? And he knew the chief of Intelligence had not been kidding. The man remembered Hamburg, and he wasn't the type to forget. If there were only some way to escape! But there wasn't. He had spent a lot of the days hours studying every square inch of his cell walls, roof, and ceiling, and, of course, the door.

No, even if the guard took his damn Mauser away from the door, he'd still be out of luck. The Germans must have hired the same building contractor who put up Alcatraz! There was only one way out of that cell. Through the door—when it was open. So why the hell wait, and suffer, and fill Peiplow's cup of revenge to overflowing?

The other half of his brain held out, however. It refused to give in and put thought into action. And so one moment he was proud of himself, and the next he cursed himself for a blithering fool. And the darkness stole all the way across Europe, and the hours dragged on and on. And they did more things than ever to his nerves, because the guard knew his stuff when it came to watching prisoners. When it got too dark to see clearly with the naked eye, he whipped out a flashlight and propped it up on the ground so that the beam held Combat right in the groove. He could do one of two things. He could close his eyes to the light, or turn his back to the door. He chose the latter and viciously commented on German guards from their ancestors right up to the present generation.

FINALLY, CLOSE to midnight, the sound of an approaching car swung Combat around on the bench. The car stopped just outside the cell door and Combat heard the voice of the Base *Kommandant* speaking from in back of that damn flashlight beam.

"Guard! Bring the prisoner out here!"

"Here it is," Combat grunted wearily as the key grated in the cell door lock. "But who the hell cares?"

The flashlight beam came into the cell, not once sliding off his face. A hand reached out and took hold of his arm in a powerful grip. The thought whipped through his brain that the guard must be holding *both* the flashlight and his rifle in his other hand. The thought died even as it was born. A second flashlight beam over by the door told him that a swing at his guard's chin would only get him death.

So he was led outside to the running board of the car. His eyes became accustomed to the dark, and he saw that the *Kommandant* was sitting in front with the driver. A guard sergeant was in back, and a guard corporal was flooding light on the running board.

"Get in back, *Herr* Captain Combat," the Commandant ordered.

The Yank hesitated and placed both hands on the door of the car.

"I'd like to ask a question," he said.

"What is the question?" the senior officer snapped.

"May I speak to the guard who has been at my cell door all day?" Combat asked.

The *Kommandant* made queer sounds in his throat.

"Eh, speak to him?" he echoed. "Yes. You have a tongue in your head, have you not? Then speak to him. He is right there at your side."

Combat turned and looked into the coarse wooden face.

"I just wanted to express my gratitude, *pal,*" he said.

And with that he drove his right fist smack into that wooden face and put every ounce of his hundred and eighty odd pounds behind it. The guard went over like a ten pin and bounced twenty feet across the ground before he stopped. By then, in fact before the others could snap out of it, Combat was in the car.

"Okay, bring on your damn firing squad!" he grated savagely.

To his surprise the *Kommandant* roared with laughter.

"Lieber Gott, you should have been born a German, *Herr* Combat!" he cried. "You know how to put dogs in their place, *nein?* The firing squad? Yes. But first, *Herr* Peiplow wishes to see you again. Yes, you are about to be honored."

THE HUMBLE driver meshed gears and got the car underway. Slouched back between the sergeant and the corporal, Combat was quite conscious of the Luger held pressed against each set of ribs. But he didn't mind, because he held no thoughts of escape. At least, not from that car. Peiplow wanted to see him again, so that meant he'd at least reach the end of this car ride alive... unless he was crazy.

So he relaxed as much as the couple of tons of German beef on either side of him would permit and tried to figure in which direction the car was going. The sky was overcast, so the North Star couldn't tell him a thing. Presently, though, the three sets of narrow gauge tracks came into the headlight beams. The car bumped across them and turned right on a dirt road that paralleled the tracks. So he knew they were headed west toward the Dutch Frontier. That made the blood leap through his veins. He had seen no sign of any flatcars or Henschels. The trick little engines had hauled them all to the other end of the tracks. And he was headed in that direction!

Presently, more tingling excitement was added to that already surging through him. The area was alive with German mechanized units. They lined both sides of the road, and were spread out across the countryside as far as he could see in the bad light. And every tank, armored car and mobile gun was expertly camouflaged. Dutch pilots patrolling their side of the fence couldn't have spotted a thing out of the way.

Mile after mile it was the same picture. Well oiled machines of sudden death on all sides. Then suddenly the car swerved to the left off the road and went bumping across the fields. Marshy ground came into the headlights, and for a moment, as the car kept right on tearing straight for it, Combat thought the driver was going to plow right on in and get bogged down up to the hubcaps.

The driver didn't, however. Fifty yards from the edge of the marsh ground, the driver turned sharp left again and braked the car to a halt. The sergeant and the corporal were very efficient. They practically lifted Combat bodily from the car and set him on his feet on the ground. And neither of them even so much as grunted. They stood waiting like a couple of wooden Indians, each with an iron grip on one of Combat's arms, while the Kommandant climbed down and started stalking off to the right. Combat was propelled along in the senior officer's wake. At what looked like a dome roofed pillbox with one side shot off, the Kommandant went down a few steps and rapped on a door.

When the summons to enter came from within, Combat was

pushed down those steps. A door opened and he was "ushered" inside on the *Kommandant's* heels. He blinked a couple of times at the sudden change of light. Then he saw that the place was fixed up pretty much like a dugout, only much more luxuriously. And the far side, directly opposite him, was flat and completely glassed over. Seated at a huge desk fitted with a dozen phones and a couple of short-wave radio panels, was Hermann Peiplow.

The chief of German Intelligence rose to his feet and bowed mockingly.

"Welcome, *Herr* Captain Combat!" he exclaimed. "Another bottle of *schnapps,* perhaps?"

CHAPTER 19
THE SECRET OF THE
SIEGFRIED LINE

C OMBAT LOOKED into the small black eyes and knew he was looking at his own death warrant, despite the friendly smile on the thick lips. He shook his head.

"No, thanks," he spoke in English. "Just tell these two apes to relax. I bruise easily."

Hermann Peiplow thought that was very funny. He roared with laughter for a moment. Then he snapped his fingers at the guards.

"Release the prisoner!" he ordered. "He does not wish to be harmed. Stand back on either side of the door, and keep your eyes open. Sit down, Captain Combat. Yes, there in the chair before me."

As the guards moved back, Combat seated himself in the chair indicated and stared at Peiplow on the other side of the desk. Though his excitement was still hitting on all cylinders, the tiny flame of hope had flickered out again. Though Peiplow was treating him like a honored guest, the German was not letting his little bit of fun over-shadow his sense of caution. He had placed the guards so that Combat sat directly in their cross-fire from behind. In other words, if he should by some miracle dart out a hand and get hold of Peiplow's Luger, he would have to whirl and shoot in two different directions in order to get the guards out of the way. That was impossible. Peiplow had him exactly where he wanted, and was loving it.

"If you will excuse me, *Herr* Peiplow," the *Kommandant* spoke up, "I will make my rounds of inspection, eh?"

The chief of German Intelligence glanced at his wristwatch and nodded.

"Yes, do that, *Herr* Colonel," he said. "The time is growing short, and *Der Fuehrer* will not want a single thing to go amiss. Yes, check again and make sure."

IMPULSIVELY COMBAT turned his head and watched the man leave. But he really turned around for a look at the two guards. Sitting in a cross-fire was right! Each guard stood fifteen feet away in a corner, his Luger and his eyes fixed on a point in the middle of Combat's back. And the eyes didn't even blink. The Yank turned front and supressed the groan that rose up in his throat. He wondered vaguely if the sergeant and the corporal would serve as the firing party when Peiplow was all through having his fun!

"Do you see the time, Captain?" Peiplow suddenly asked, and thrust forward his wristwatch. "It is a little before two o'clock in the morning. Do you know what day it is, eh?"

"Saturday, unless I've skipped a day somewhere," Combat grunted.

"Saturday, yes," Peiplow nodded. "Saturday, the Eleventh. The Eleventh of November!"

The German's eyes glittered as he spoke the last. Combat sucked in his breath sharply and sat up a bit in his chair.

"Yeah, Armistice Day!" he murmured. "And my birthday, too! Damned if it isn't!"

"My felicitations, Captain," the German said and bowed mockingly. "It is indeed a day for the history books. The day of Germany's great humiliation twenty-one years ago. Your birthday. And now, the birthday of the greatest Germany of all. Do you know how I shall celebrate it?"

"I could guess," Combat grunted, "but let it pass."

"I shall celebrate by eating my dinner tonight—in Amsterdam!" Peiplow popped at him.

"You *hope!*" Combat popped back.

"I *know!*" the German corrected. "But you do not seem surprised. Perhaps you have guessed, eh, from what little you were able to learn?"

"I guess I had the general idea figured out," Combat shrugged. "It's not such a bad pipe-dream, at that. But just how do you figure you're going to make it work?"

The German chuckled softly, picked up a pan of dirt that rested on a corner of the desk and placed it in front of him.

"THAT IS exactly why I have invited you here, Captain," he smiled crookedly at the Yank. "Your English press does not think kindly toward me, but as I have already told you, I am a great admirer of courage, whether it be in friend or foe. Courage should always be rewarded. This is the manner in which I desire to reward you. You came to Germany to find out something, Captain. You tried hard but you failed—shall we say, miserably? But courageous effort must be rewarded, so I am going to show you what you didn't find out. I am going to let you see the German forces in actual operation. And then I am going to have you shot by those two guards in back of you."

The German paused and made a slight gesture of contrition.

"Forgive me if my thoroughness displeases you, Captain," he mocked. "I believe in being thorough, however. I must make sure that my own eyes see you die. Then I will know. For a little while, though, you may be interested. Of course, if you become bored—well, naturally, the two guards are at your service."

Peiplow chuckled at his little joke and picked up a pen, a pencil, a few paper clips, and the composition cap off the inkwell. All these he dumped into the pan of dirt on the desk. Then, pulling open a drawer, he took out two small glass bottles of perhaps three ounce capacity each. One contained a pale blue crystalline powder. The other contained powder that was pure white. Peiplow set them on the desk before him and smiled at Combat.

"Before I make my little demonstration," he said, "let me forestall your inevitable question. I am not a chemist, and so I do not know the—er—ingredients that make up these two powders. The secret of that is safe in the files of the Bureau of

Scientific War Research. I only know what they will do. Now, I will show you."

Picking up the bottle of pale blue powder, Peiplow took off the cap and sprinkled a tiny bit of the stuff on the dirt-filled tray. So small an amount did Peiplow sprinkle that had Combat not watched closely he would have sworn that every speck of the powder was still in the bottle. Placing the bottle to one side, Peiplow picked up the other bottle, unscrewed its cap, and held it dramatically poised over the tray of dirt.

"Watch, my dear Captain Combat!" he said hoarsely.

Perhaps four specks of the white powder, but not more, spilled out of the bottle and down into the tray. His eyes fixed on the tray, Peiplow hastily recapped the bottle and put it to one side, with the other. But even as he made the movement the tray of dirt gave forth a soft hissing sound. In another second it had become a pool of glowing red that gave forth neither smoke nor tongues of flame. It spread over the dirt and fused the various articles Peiplow had placed there. As Combat stared, fascinated, the red glow died out and there was nothing left but a film of ashes and scorched dirt. The pencil, pen, paper clips, and inkwell top were gone.

"It was very pretty, eh?"

Hermann Peiplow's voice snapped Combat out of his trance, and pulled his thoughts for a moment to the North Sea, when a Henschel had gone slipping over that lumbering tramp steamer. There before him, on Peiplow's desk, was a miniature example of what had happened to that tramp steamer. With an effort he raised his eyes to Peiplow's and grinned.

"Do I clap now, or is there more?" he asked lightly.

The German's flat face flushed a beet crimson, and his two hands resting on the desk clenched into rock-hard fists. For a second Combat regretted making the hollow crack. If Peiplow went haywire, two Luger bullets would race for the middle of his back. The German quickly regained control of his rage, however. He smiled broadly.

"Of course there is more, my dear Captain," he said smoothly. "You have just seen what a tiny bit of those chemicals can do. Turn your head and glance out the window."

COMBAT AUTOMATICALLY clamped down hard on his nerves, and obeyed. He was mildly surprised to see there was considerable dawn light outside, but his heart stood still at what else he saw. Some thirty-five feet beyond the window were three oblong cement blocks sunk almost to a level with the ground. A set of narrow gauge tracks ran right up to the rear end of each block. Fitted to each block was airplane launching gear, and resting on the gear, tail up in flying position, was one of the Henschel planes. The launching release cord was strung to the pilot's cockpit so that he could launch himself whenever he was ready.

Beside each plane were two or three tanks. Coils led from these tanks to the smaller tanks fitted under the belly of each ship. Hun mechanics were fussing around them, turning knobs, pulling levers, and adjusting gauge dials. The three sets of tracks extended back beyond his range of vision, but on all three were flatcars, and on each flatcar was another Henschel. In short, as each plane was launched, the one behind it was trundled into place on the launching gear. The planes carried no observer, but a helmeted pilot sat in each ship. The three Henschels on the launching blocks had their props turning over slowly.

Combat stared, and Peiplow's voice seemed to come to him from another world.

"You are looking at the reason I know I shall eat my dinner in Amsterdam tonight, Captain," the German was saying. "Those planes out there. Yes, what you are probably thinking is entirely correct. That is specially designed dusting apparatus that you see. However, you will note there are two outlets at the tail. That is for a reason you can guess. The chemicals are kept in separate tanks. They do not merge until they have left the outlets. Being not dust, and considerably heavier than air, they sink to the ground at once. There they mix with the *known* chemicals in the ground. And the result—is a hundred million times greater than what I have just shown you! And, of course, the Dutch border is only five miles away, in case you are wondering."

Combat made no comment. He was too choked up inside to have been able to speak a word, even at the point of a gun. Hermann Peiplow didn't have to tell him any more. The picture, the secret of the Siegfried Line, was complete. Nothing was missing, now.

At zero hour German troops in the Siegfried Line would be hurled against the mighty Maginot defenses. Hundreds—hell, thousands would be killed, but that wouldn't matter a damn. It would keep the Allied forces busy, and that was the main idea. Because at the same zero hour those Henschels outside would be launched in groups of three. With their death dusting equipment they would literally burn a five mile highway straight across Holland to the sea, destroying everything—leveling everything flat. And close behind would come Hitler's mighty mechanized armies. Thundering and booming straight forward. Units of the left and right flanks would stop the Dutch and Belgian forces cold, while the main part of the armies rolled right down the center.

Three hours at the most, and the Germans would be in Amsterdam. The Maginot and Belgian Lines would be flanked. German pursuit planes, reconnaissance ships, and bombers would roar squadron after squadron to Amsterdam's airdromes, leaving the low countries cut squarely in two, and the German hordes right on the English Channel. France completely cut off from her ally. Hitler's butchers in a position to pounce down upon England at will....

Combat groaned aloud, half twisted his body and slumped over Peiplow's desk and buried his head in his arms.

"Oh, dear God, don't let them!" he moaned. *"Don't let them!"*

CHAPTER 20
EAGLES NEVER LINGER

THE INTERIOR of the dugout rang with Peiplow's wild laughter. He thumped his fists on the edge of the desk in berserk glee.

"Look at him, now!" he bellowed. "The great Captain Combat! A sniveling, whimpering dog. You would believe you were more clever than I, *dummköpfe?* Me, Hermann Peiplow?

Lieber Gott, all of your breed are swine fools. Look some more, Captain! Did I not say I would reward you? Let you see for yourself? *Ach,* this is so much better than having you shot yesterday when they caught you. *Ja,* this is a day I shall always remember. I shall think of how you look now, this very instant. And I shall think of the thoughts that are pouring through your brain, now. It will be very beautiful to think back on all this. Go on, look some more. You have a little longer to live. Ja, you have until the Zero Hour when the first three planes will be launched. Seventeen minutes, to be exact. So have your fill of looking, Captain, and enjoy it while you may!"

Arms half sprawled across the desk, and his head resting on them, Bill Combat prayed as he had never prayed before. Then he raised his head, quickly dragged his hands down off the desk, and sat up straight. Tears of laughter were running down Peiplow's cheeks. He looked into Combat's face, and what he saw there seemed somehow not to be funny. There were not tears in Combat's eyes. They were cold, hard, agate.

"Do your guards speak English, or understand it, Peiplow?" he asked in his own language.

The German blinked, then snorted.

"No," he said. "What difference does it make? They shoot when I give them the word."

"Maybe you're not going to give the word to shoot," Combat said grimly. "You're not the only ham actor around this joint, pal. I'm not so bad myself. If you want to die, Peiplow, just start getting all excited. Just let out one peep at those guards. Take a look *at my hands,* Peiplow!"

The German blinked again, then lowered his gaze to Combat's hands.

"Easy, Peiplow!" Combat warned as the German started to tremble. "Put the brakes on, or else, so help me!"

With a mighty effort the German got control of himself, but his eyes remained fastened upon the two hands Combat held slightly in front of his chest so they were hidden from both of the guards. And no wonder Peiplow held his gaze on those two hands, because in the right was the bottle of pale blue crystalline powder. And in the left hand was the bottle of pure white powder. Yes, for the infinitesimal part of a second the German's gaze flickered away from those hands. He swept a glance across his desk just to make sure. It was true! The hand is quicker than the eye....

"No, I never throw myself about like a school girl, when I'm unhappy, Peiplow," Combat said evenly. "Draping over your desk was just part of the act. Now look, Peiplow, I can smack these bottles together, bust them, and this place will get hot as hell. So...."

"Mein Gott, don't, Combat!" the German breathed.

"Not unless you make me," Combat said evenly. "And get this before you even start thinking. Maybe you have some high sign those two square heads in back of me can catch, and I won't even know it. But note how I'm holding these bottles. Whichever way I fall they'll bust... and it won't help *you* a bit. I'm not saying the guards can't shoot me, Peiplow. They can! But these bottles will be busted before I'm dead, and we'll all show up in hell plenty singed. Okay, give them the high sign, if you want to."

Combat grinned tight-lipped when he finished, but his heart was standing still. In fact, heaven and earth were standing still as far as he was concerned. If he had tabbed Peiplow's breed wrong, he was going to be a dead man pretty soon. But, if he had tabbed the German right, he had the slim chance to save Europe, and perhaps his own life. It all depended upon Hermann Peiplow, oddly enough. Was he, or wasn't he?

The German's wrist watch ticked off fifteen seconds, and each faint tick was like cannon fire in Combat's ears as he sat there waiting. And then suddenly the battle of emotions that had been fought in the German's small black eyes was at an end. Hermann Peiplow *was!* He was yellow at the core. Like each of the blustering blowhards of the Nazi regime, their own life was the most precious thing in the Third Reich. And they would instantly sacrifice anybody else's life to keep it.

"You can do nothing," Peiplow said in a flat, stale beer-like voice. "You will never leave here alive. It is too late to do anything. Too late, I tell you!"

"A guy can always try," Combat said softly. "Okay, Peiplow, call your guards over here, and tell them to put their guns on the desk. I'm standing up."

COMBAT'S HEART was a long ways from its usual place as he slowly rose to his feet, hugging the two bottles. But he had to be on his feet in order to make yardage on the next play. Peiplow hesitated the fraction of a second, but when Combat purposely let his two hands shake, it was more than the Hun could take.

"Guards!" he snarled in his native tongue. "Come over here and place your guns on the desk, and stand at attention."

Out the corner of his eye Combat saw the dazed expression that spread on the face of each guard. Then they clicked their heels and advanced to obey the order. No sooner had they placed their guns on the table than Combat shifted the bottle in his right hand to his left, scooped up one of the guns and slid around in back of the guards. Each trembled, expecting an order from Peiplow's thick lips, but the chief of German Intelligence sat motionless in his chair. Then both guards stopped trembling. They did because in one continuous movement Combat clipped them both hard on the back of the head with the Luger barrel. They fell to the floor like a couple of fence posts. Very neatly, too. One to the right, and one to the left. Combat stepped between them grinning at Peiplow.

"And now that leaves only you, *pal!*" he grated. "Be a nice boy and tilt your skull this way. Yup, I'm going to give you the break you gave me. Fair is fair, you know. So I'm going to let you live a little longer. Come on, tilt it, sweetheart!"

The veins at the German's temples stood out. His neck cords were stiff, and his eyes bleak with savage hate. He stared Combat straight in the eye for a full five seconds and then slowly started to bend his head forward. Perhaps, though, in that brief moment a tiny spark of soldier's courage did spring into life within him, and he was willing to risk his life for his native land.

At any rate, Hermann Peiplow suddenly lunged his huge bulk across the desk top. His great paws were outstretched and one of them he clamped about Combat's left hand holding the bottle.

Then he went slanting down
on more of Hitler's troops.

Then he brought his face down and buried his teeth in the flesh of Combat's wrist. White pain shot clean up the Yank's arm to his shoulder socket, and he almost let go of the two bottles. But he clung to them despite the teeth and the fingernails digging into his wrist and hand. And at the same time he brought the Luger down on the top of Peiplow's thick skull.

Had he hit any harder the gun barrel would probably have snapped right off. Hermann Peiplow immediately relaxed, lurched back, then slumped down to bury his face in the pan of scorched dirt and stay still. And at that very instant the engines of the three Henschels on the launching blocks outside roared up in full throated song.

Zero hour had come!

Spinning around on one heel, Combat leaped for the dugout door, and yanked it open. He went pounding up the short flight of steps to crash straight into the figure of the Base Commander hurrying down them. Instinctively Combat squeezed the trigger of the Luger he still clutched. The gun spat flame, and a bullet right into the Base Commander's stomach. The man reeled and fell heavily against Combat. In wrenching himself free the Yank lost his grip on the Luger. It was knocked from his hand and went clattering down the dugout steps. He came close to tripping and going down the steps on his ear after it.

Somehow he managed to regain his balance. But he didn't bother to twist around and duck down after the gun. There wasn't time. Two of the death dusting planes had already shot off their launching blocks, and the third pilot was getting set to let himself go, too. Combat switched the two bottles to his

146

right hand, bent over almost double and tore straight toward that last plane.

Off to his left, somebody let go a wild bellow of alarm. He gave one flash glance in that direction and saw the group of officers and pilots standing back waiting for the third plane to leave. Without slackening his pace, Combat jerked up his right hand and slung both bottles at the nose of the Henschel resting on its little flat car directly in back of the one on the launching blocks. The bottles hit the metal cowling and broke just as Combat was diving through the air toward the cockpit of the first Henschel.

Its pilot, reaching for the launching cord, froze stiff for a second, and stared, wild-eyed. Then it was too late for him to grab the launching cord and yank. Combat's diving body hit him like six ton of bricks tossed off the top of the Empire State. The German pilot went out like a light, but Combat didn't know that. He brought up his right clenched fist under the German's jaw. Naturally, the man didn't feel his jawbone snap in three places.

Conscious that voices were screaming in agony behind him, and that hissing red hell was coming his way, Combat called on every ounce of his strength and lifted the German pilot bodily out of the pit and let him drop. Then he dived into the vacated seat, grabbed the stick, slapped his feet on the rudder pedals, and yanked the launching cord. As though an invisible giant had suddenly booted the Henschel in the tail, the plane shot off the launching block, just as a terrific blast of heat swiped against the back of Combat's neck.

IT SEEMED to dry up the blood in his veins, to shrivel

his heart, and to burn the air right under his lungs. For several seconds he was unable to move a muscle. Unable to do a thing as the plane went lurching crazily forward not more than a dozen feet or so off the ground. Then strength and the power to act surged back into his body. He hauled back the stick and pulled the nose of the Henschel toward the sky. At five hundred feet he kicked rudder and swung around toward the east.

Below and a bit ahead were the launching blocks. They and the hundred square yards or so of area about them were covered with a gleaming red shroud that spread out slowly like spilled molasses on a brown and green rug. He couldn't pick out where the dugout was, and as he went tearing down, his free hand gripping the "dusting" release valve handle, Combat wondered if Hermann Peiplow was buried under that gleaming smoke-less hell fury.

"Here's hoping!" he shouted and tightened his grip on the release valve handle. "But I doubt it like hell! His breed some how always manages to cheat their pal, the Devil!"

With a nod for emphasis he went swooping down over a scene of utter terrified confusion such as had never before been witnessed in the wars of the world. Whether they knew it, or simply suspected that something had gone damn wrong, every one of the thousands and thousands of Germans in the sector suddenly went haywire in an effort to get away. Men, tanks, armored cars, mobile guns, and Henschel plane pilots began milling around like a gigantic swarm of angry bees.

"Tough!" Combat shouted and leveled off no more than fifty feet above the ground. "Tough as hell… you stinking rats!"

And with that he pulled the release valve handle. For a moment nothing happened, and fear struck him that there was more to do than just pull the handle. But suddenly he heard harshing hissing sound that came to his ears above the thunder of the plane's powerful BMW engine. He twisted his head and looked down past the tail. A blanket of crystalline blue, mixed with pure white, was dropping down upon the wild confusion below. It touched earth like a heavy fog, and then the crystalline blue and the pure white changed into a glistening red flame that lapped outward to the sides instead of licking upward. And everything it touched, men, guns, tanks, and all the other things disappeared from sight once they were bathed in that burning, smokeless substance of complete devastation.

"God!" Combat breathed and clenched his teeth hard. "God, I can almost feel sorry for those stinking sons of Satan. Only I don't!"

Closing the release valve he zoomed for altitude, then cut toward the north and went slanting down upon more of Hitler's mechanized units. Back and forth he tore across the entire area, sparing nothing and no one with his savage, devastating attack. Then finally the entire area was swamped in the glistening red hell.

"Try it again some other time, you bums!" he bellowed down at the panorama of death and destruction. "Just try it again sometime and I'll damn...."

He choked off the rest as he happened to glance upward. His heart banged up into his throat to stick fast against his rear teeth. In his wild efforts to wipe out Hitler's "surprise" armies he had completely forgotten about the two Henschels that had managed to get launched. Their pilots had streaked for the Dutch frontier and had started to lay down their curtain of glistening hell only to find that they were all alone. So they had turned back, obviously, to find out what had gone wrong. They had found out, and now they were striving to spray death down upon the man who had turned glorious triumph into complete disaster for the Nazi horde.

In short, the two Henschels were tearing down to flatten out over Combat and spray him. And in another split second they would be in position to do just that. A yell of alarm bursting off his lips, Combat hurled his ship over on its wing, kicked the nose earthward and started straight down toward the carpet of glistening red below. The instant the rising blast of terrific heat struck him he flattened out and shot straight forward until he could stand the heat no longer. Then he zoomed up and toward the west.

The Two Henschels had followed him down in the dive and they were close behind as he shot up in his zoom. But that's how he wanted it to be. He had to chance that they'd use their guns. Perhaps, though, they didn't want to use their guns; wanted to get Combat the way he got their swastika buddies. At any rate they tried to get even closer, and in so doing barged straight into Combat's trap. As he went zooming up, the Yank pulled the valve release handle. Mixed death hissed out from the tail of his plane. He pulled back the stick all the more and went curving up in the first half of a mighty loop. Hanging head down, he watched the two Henschel pilots strive frantically to swerve clear of the band of white and blue that Combat had traced in the sky. One of them succeeded, but the other was out of luck. He flew straight into the stuff, fell over on one wing and dived straight into the ground to disappear from view.

ROLLING OFF the top of his loop to a right-side-up position, Combat waited until his band of death had sunk to the ground. Then he dropped his nose and went wing howling down after the lone Henschel whose pilot now had nothing on his mind but a desire to get away.

"Not even you, pal!" Combat shouted and slid his thumbs up to the trigger trips.

"But you're getting a break. You're going out the way a pilot should go out. Yeah, with slugs in his hide!"

Though it will never be known for truth, perhaps, it is possible that the gods of war caught Combat's shouted words out of the air and poured them into the ears of that fleeing Nazi pilot.

Anyway, the Henschel suddenly came swiping around on wing tip and charged straight up at Combat with all four guns blazing.

"I'll be damned!" Combat yelped and jabbed his own trigger trips forward. "Something new every day in this cockeyed war. There's a Hun who actually wants a man-to-man scrap, and not odds!"

With each word that skipped off his lips, Combat punctuated it with a savage blast of fire. The German pilot tried desperately to return the fire with good results. And for a few seconds he succeeded. One burst bounced off Combat's engine cowling, and another burst went by his ears so close he could hear each bullet say, "Howdy!" Then the German pilot stopped shooting because you can't shoot aerial machine guns when you're dead. You can't fly an airplane either! The Henschel staggered over on one wing, hovered there for a moment and then dropped down to add a bit more fuel to the sea of flame below.

No sooner had it started down than Combat kicked his ship around and headed straight for the Dutch border. He would have flown south down toward France, but a glance in that direction showed a flock of dots in the sky. Perhaps they were Allied planes on their way up, but he was pretty sure they were German bombers on their way north to join a party that wasn't going to be pulled off.

Anyway, Combat went tearing west across the Dutch frontier, and the Dutch anti-aircraft gunners started banging away at him... not realizing, of course. For thirty minutes or so he had the most uncomfortable flight of his life. It doesn't make you feel happy to have lads you're not sore at all bang away at you in earnest. Finally, though, the city of Amsterdam came sliding up over the western horizon. More anti aircraft guns greeted him there, and he looked longingly down at the inviting landing fields below. But he shook his head, and pushed out over the waters of the English Channel.

"I wouldn't want you to be forced to intern me, friends!" he shouted back over his shoulder. "Besides, Sir John is probably all hot and bothered waiting for me. He...."

Bill Combat never did finish that sentence. The BMW engine in the nose stopped him cold. Stopped him cold because it began to cough and sputter badly. Instinctively Combat's eye flew to the gas gauge on the instrument dial. It showed empty, and he knew that but one thing could have caused that situation. And it wasn't because the engine had lapped up a full tank of gas. No, that last Henschel pilot had managed to leave a little something for Combat to remember. In a few words, a neat little bullet hole in the gas tank. And now the last of the gas had leaked out. The dial needle went hard against the zero peg, and the engine even stopped its sputtering and coughing.

"And that's that!" Combat grunted and glanced back toward shore.

IT WAS about five miles away and with a bit of luck he might reach it in a flat glide. But that would mean he'd be interned. He shook his head and stared to the west. And finally Lady Luck did come back. A British patrol destroyer was churning the waves in his direction. Even as he spotted it the craft's forward deck anti-aircraft guns banged into action. Combat jumped, promptly stuck the nose down and went hell bent for the water.

He leveled off as fast as he could and made a splash landing. The destroyer came barging up, hoved to alongside, and with the aid of half a dozen sailors and a couple of boathooks he was hauled up on deck. He heaved a long sigh of relief as his feet touched British "territory." Yes, it would have been nice to have reached England with that dusting Henschel. The Air Ministry would be plenty interested to have a look. But... But to hell with it, now.

"This is the second time your destroyer lads have fished me out of the water," he grinned at the commander who stood regarding him cold eyed. "Maybe I should get transferred to the navy."

HALF AN hour later Combat sat in the commander's cabin as the destroyer bowled along for the English coast. Radio messages had been dispatched to all the proper people at the proper places, and for the first time in a hundred years, or so it seemed to Combat, he could really relax and not care a damn. He accepted the whiskey bottle the commander pushed toward him and poured five fingers into his glass. As he started to raise it to his lips he noticed the spots of blood and little gashes made by Hermann Peiplow's teeth on his left hand. He regarded them with a frown, and then deliberately spilled some of the whiskey over the hand.

The destroyer commander gasped and almost fell out of his chair.

"I say, what the devil?" he cried. "That's good whiskey, man!"

"An old American custom, Commander," Combat grinned. "There's nothing like good whiskey for snake bite. Externally *and* internally."

And with that Bill Combat poured the rest of the whiskey slowly down his throat.

POPULAR HERO PULPS AVAILABLE NOW:

THE SPIDER
- ❏ #1: The Spider Strikes — $13.95
- ❏ #2: The Wheel of Death — $13.95
- ❏ #3: Wings of the Black Death — $13.95
- ❏ #4: City of Flaming Shadows — $13.95
- ❏ #5: Empire of Doom! — $13.95
- ❏ #6: Citadel of Hell — $13.95
- ❏ #7: The Serpent of Destruction — $13.95
- ❏ #8: The Mad Horde — $13.95
- ❏ #9: Satan's Death Blast — $13.95
- ❏ #10: The Corpse Cargo — $13.95
- ❏ #11: Prince of the Red Looters — $13.95
- ❏ #12: Reign of the Silver Terror — $13.95
- ❏ #13: Builders of the Dark Empire — $13.95
- ❏ #14: Death's Crimson Juggernaut — $13.95
- ❏ #15: The Red Death Rain — $13.95
- ❏ #16: The City Destroyer — $13.95
- ❏ #17: The Pain Emperor — $13.95
- ❏ #18: The Flame Master — $13.95
- ❏ #19: Slaves of the Crime Master — $13.95
- ❏ #20: Reign of the Death Fiddler — $13.95
- ❏ #21: Hordes of the Red Butcher — $13.95
- ❏ #22: Dragon Lord of the Underworld — $13.95
- ❏ #23: Master of the Death-Madness — $13.95
- ❏ #24: King of the Red Killers — $13.95
- ❏ #25: Overlord of the Damned — $13.95
- ❏ #26: Death Reign of the Vampire King — $13.95
- ❏ #27: Emperor of the Yellow Death — $13.95
- ❏ #28: The Mayor of Hell — $13.95
- ❏ #29: Slaves of the Murder Syndicate — $13.95
- ❏ #30: Green Globes of Death — $13.95
- ❏ #31: The Cholera King — $13.95
- ❏ #32: Slaves of the Dragon — $13.95
- ❏ #33: Legions of Madness — $12.95
- ❏ #34: Laboratory of the Damned — $12.95
- ❏ #35: Satan's Sightless Legion — $12.95
- ❏ #36: The Coming of the Terror — $12.95
- ❏ #37: The Devil's Death-Dwarfs — $12.95
- ❏ #38: City of Dreadful Night — $12.95
- ❏ #39: Reign of the Snake Men — $12.95
- ❏ #40: Dictator of the Damned — $12.95
- ❏ #41: The Mill-Town Massacres — $12.95
- ❏ #42: Satan's Workshop — $12.95
- ❏ #43: Scourge of the Yellow Fangs — $12.95
- ❏ #44: The Devil's Pawnbroker — $12.95
- ❏ #45: Voyage of the Coffin Ship — $12.95
- ❏ #46: The Man Who Ruled in Hell — $13.95
- ❏ #47: Slaves of the Black Monarch — $13.95
- ❏ #48: Machineguns Over the White House — $13.95
- ❏ #49: The City That Dared Not Eat — $13.95
- ❏ #50: Master of the Flaming Horde — $13.95
- ❏ #51: Satan's Switchboard — $13.95
- ❏ #52: Legions of the Accursed Light — $13.95
- ❏ #53: The City of Lost Men — $13.95
- ❏ *NEW:* #54: The Grey Horde Creeps — $13.95

THE WESTERN RAIDER
- ❏ #1: Guns of the Damned — $13.95
- ❏ #2: The Hawk Rides Back from Death — $13.95
- ❏ #3: Gun-Call for the Lost Legion — $13.95
- ❏ #4: The Law of Silver Trent — $13.95
- ❏ #5: The Gun-Prayer of Silver Trent — $13.95
- ❏ #6: Silver Trent Rides Alone — $13.95

G-8 AND HIS BATTLE ACES
- ❏ #1: The Bat Staffel — $13.95

CAPTAIN SATAN
- ❏ #1: The Mask of the Damned — $13.95
- ❏ #2: Parole for the Dead — $13.95
- ❏ #3: The Dead Man Express — $13.95
- ❏ #4: A Ghost Rides the Dawn — $13.95
- ❏ #5: The Ambassador From Hell — $13.95

DR. YEN SIN
- ❏ #1: Mystery of the Dragon's Shadow — $12.95
- ❏ #2: Mystery of the Golden Skull — $12.95
- ❏ #3: Mystery of the Singing Mummies — $12.95